"So, you're offering to…what? Be my personal bodyguard?"

"In an unofficial capacity," Joshua replied.

Savannah had managed to minimize the danger of last night since she'd awakened this morning, but his offer of bodyguard services put a new spin on things.

"Are you sure that's necessary?" she asked.

"No, I'm not sure about much of anything. But I've always thought it was better to be safe than sorry."

"If we're talking about my safety, then I like the way you think," she said with a touch of dry humor. She wasn't sure what made her more uncomfortable, the way her heart pounded at the thought that she might be in danger, or her heart's reaction to the thought of having Joshua at her side for the next couple days.

Carla Cassidy

THE BODYGUARD'S
RETURN

Silhouette®

INTIMATE MOMENTS™

Published by Silhouette Books

America's Publisher of Contemporary Romance

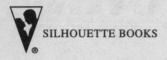

SILHOUETTE BOOKS

ISBN-13: 978-0-373-27517-5
ISBN-10:   0-373-27517-X

THE BODYGUARD'S RETURN

Visit Silhouette Books at www.eHarlequin.com

Printed in U.S.A.

Books by Carla Cassidy

Silhouette Intimate Moments

*The Delaney Heirs
‡‡Cherokee Corners
†Wild West Bodyguards

CARLA CASSIDY

is an award-winning author who has written over fifty novels for Silhouette Books. In 1995 she won Best Silhouette Romance from *Romantic Times BOOKreviews* for *Anything for Danny*. In 1998 she also won a Career Achievement Award for Best Innovative Series from *Romantic Times BOOKreviews*.

Carla believes the only thing better than curling up with a good book to read is sitting down at the computer with a good story to write. She's looking forward to writing many more books and bringing hours of pleasure to readers.

Chapter 1

She'd never meant to make Cotter Creek, Oklahoma, her home. Savannah Marie Clarion had been on her way to nowhere when the transmission in her car had decided to go wonky. She'd managed to pull it into Mechanic's Mansion on Main Street before it had died completely.

She'd taken one look around the dusty small town and had decided Cotter Creek sure felt like nowhere to her.

That had been three months ago. She now hurried down Main Street toward the Sunny Side Up Café where she was meeting Meredith West for lunch. After that she had an interview to conduct for her job as a reporter for the *Cotter Creek Chronicle,* the daily newspaper.

"Good morning, Mr. Rhenquist." She smiled at the old man who sat in a chair in front of the barbershop. His deeply weathered face looked like the cracked Oklahoma earth as he scowled at her.

"Somebody eat the bottom of your britches?" he asked.

She flashed him a bright smile. "It's the latest style, Mr. Rhenquist. They're cropped short on purpose."

"Looks silly to me," he replied. "No place for fashion in Cotter Creek."

"If they ever ban grouchy old farts from Cotter Creek, you'd better pack your bags," she retorted. She instantly bit her lower lip and hurried on, trying not to feel self-conscious in the short gray pants, sleek black boots and pink sweater that clashed cheerfully with her bright red curly hair.

She could almost hear her mother's voice ringing in her ears as she hurried toward the café. "You're brash, Savannah Marie. You're outspoken and it's quite unbecoming."

She stuffed her mother's voice in the mental box where she kept all the unpleasantness of her life as she entered the Sunny Side Up Café. She was greeted by the lingering breakfast scents of fried bacon and strong coffee now being overwhelmed by burgers and onions and the lunchtime fare.

Immediately she spied Meredith at a booth near

the back of the busy café. At the sight of her friend, Savannah couldn't help the smile that curved her lips.

Meredith West had been one of the first people Savannah had met when she'd settled into the upstairs of a house owned by Ms. Winnie Halifax. Meredith had been visiting the sweet old lady when Savannah had been moving in.

On the surface Savannah and Meredith couldn't be more different. Meredith always looked like she'd dressed in the dark, pulling on whatever her hands managed to land on while still half-asleep. On the other hand, Savannah had been breast-fed fashion sense by a superficial mother who had believed physical beauty was the second most important thing to being rich.

"Don't you look spiffy," Meredith said as Savannah slid into the booth opposite her.

"Thanks. Rhenquist just asked me what happened to the bottom of my britches."

Meredith's full lips curved into a smile. "Rhenquist is an old boob."

A young waitress appeared at their table to take their order, interrupting their conversation momentarily. "So, what's up with you?" Savannah asked when the waitress had left their booth. "Are you off on another adventure?"

Meredith worked for the family business, Wild West Protective Services. Savannah had been intrigued when she'd learned her new friend worked as a bodyguard. "And when are you going to let me interview you for my column?"

"No, and never," Meredith replied. "I've decided to take some time off." She leaned forward, her green eyes sparkling. "My brother, Joshua is coming home. He should be here sometime today or tomorrow."

"You have too many brothers. Which one is Joshua?"

"The baby. He's been in New York for the past year and a half and we've all missed him desperately." Her affection for her younger sibling was obvious in her voice.

"Is this a visit?"

"No, he's decided to move back here. He says he's had enough of the big city. He'd probably love for you to interview him. Joshua has never shied away from attention."

"I'll keep that in mind," Savannah replied. "I'm interviewing Charlie Summit this afternoon."

"Now that should be interesting. I can't believe Cotter Creek's epitome of crazy as a loon is going to talk to you." Meredith shoved a strand of her long dark hair behind one ear.

"Actually, beneath his gruff exterior and eccentricities, Charlie is a very nice man. I sometimes go over to his place in the evenings and we play chess together. He's lonely and he was thrilled when I told him I wanted to talk to him for one of my 'People and Personality' columns."

"When we were kids he used to scare the hell out of us," Meredith said after the waitress had returned to serve their orders. "He lived all alone out there in the middle of nowhere and looked like Grizzly Adams on a bad day. There was a rumor that his root cellar was filled with children who had disobeyed their parents."

Savannah laughed. "I wonder who started that particular rumor?"

"Probably some parent with disobedient children."

Meredith paused to take a sip of her iced tea, then continued. "Actually, Joshua became good friends with him when Joshua was about fifteen years old. You know that weather vane that Charlie has stuck in the ground next to his house?"

"You mean that copper monstrosity with the rooster?"

Meredith nodded. "One night a bunch of Joshua's friends dared him to steal it. Joshua sneaked up and Charlie was waiting for him with a shotgun in hand."

"So, what happened?"

"Charlie made Joshua go inside the house and call my father. As punishment Joshua had to go over to Charlie's twice a week after school and work. I think he's kept in touch with Charlie even while he's been in New York."

"If your brother is his friend, that makes two friends for Charlie. I'm hoping my article on him will humanize him and make people look beyond the scruffy beard and gruff exterior."

"Oh, I almost forgot." Meredith opened her purse and pulled out a cream-colored envelope and handed it across the table to Savannah.

"What's this?"

"A wedding invitation. Clay and Libby are getting married a week from next Saturday."

"Wow, that's kind of fast, isn't it?" Savannah knew a little about the romance between Meredith's brother Clay and the beautiful blonde from Hollywood.

Clay had been sent to Hollywood to play bodyguard to Libby's daughter, Gracie, who was a little movie star and had been receiving threatening notes in the mail. Clay and Libby had fallen in love, and Libby and her daughter had moved to Cotter Creek a couple of weeks ago.

Meredith smiled, a touch of wistfulness in her eyes. "Yes, it's fast, but, according to Clay and Libby, when you know something is right you don't waste any time."

The two women continued to visit as they ate their lunch, then all too quickly it was time for Savannah to head to her interview with Charlie.

It was almost one o'clock as Savannah drove down Main Street, headed to the outskirts of town and the small ranch house where Charlie Summit lived.

Every morning for the past three months she had awakened and been vaguely surprised to discover herself for the most part content with her new life.

And content was something she couldn't ever remember feeling in her twenty-four years of life.

Savannah had awakened one morning in her beautiful bedroom in her parents' beautiful house and had realized if she didn't get away from the criticism and unrealistic expectations she'd never know who she was and what she was capable of being.

And so she'd headed for the biggest adventure of her life…finding her life.

It had been that faulty transmission that had brought her to Cotter Creek and a further stroke of luck that Raymond Buchannan, the owner of the local newspaper, was getting old and tired. When she'd approached him with her journalism degree in one hand and an idea for profiling the locals in a column each week in the other, he'd hired her.

In the time she'd been here, she'd grown to love Cotter Creek, but she'd begun to think something bad was happening here. There had been too many accidental deaths of local ranchers lately. On a whim she'd done some research and the results were troubling, to say the least.

She shoved away thoughts of those deaths and rolled down her window to allow in the crisp early-October air, so different from the desert heat in Scottsdale, Arizona, where she'd grown up.

She was looking forward to the interview with Charlie. All her teachers in her journalism classes had told her that she was particularly good at the art of interviewing.

She always managed to glean one little nugget of information that exposed the very center of a person. It was one of her strengths. Her mother had spent her lifetime cataloging Savannah's weaknesses.

Charlie Summit lived, as most of the ranchers in the area did, in the middle of nowhere. But, unlike most of the flat pastures of his neighbors, Charlie's little two-bedroom ranch house was surrounded by woods and a yard that hadn't seen the blade of a lawnmower in the past twenty years.

A rusted-out pickup truck body sat on cinder blocks on the east side of the house, surrounded by old scraps of tin and the infamous, huge, elaborate copper weather vane.

The junkyard collection, coupled with his hermit-like tendencies, certainly helped add to Charlie's reputation as an odd duck.

What was definitely odd was that, as Savannah pulled her car to a halt in front of the overgrown path that led to Charlie's front door, his two dogs, Judd and Jessie, were pacing the porch, obviously agitated.

Charlie never let the dogs stay out on their own. He'd always told her the two mutts were too dumb to know to scratch an itch unless he was sitting beside them telling them how to do it.

As she got out of her car, the two came running to her. They raced around her feet, releasing sharp whines. "What's the matter, boys?" she asked and knelt down to pet first the tall, mostly golden retriever then the smaller, mostly fox terrier. Savannah loved dogs, one of her many character flaws where her parents were concerned.

She stood and looked toward the house, where the front door was open, but no sound drifted outward. Odd. Charlie never left his door open. He'd always told her that an open door invited in trouble.

The curly red hairs on the nape of her neck sprang to attention as a sense of apprehension slithered through her,

"Charlie?" she called as she stepped closer to the porch. Judd and Jessie whined at her feet. "Charlie, it's me, Savannah."

She climbed the steps and paused at the front door as she caught a whiff of a scent that didn't belong. It smelled like a firecracker seconds after explosion. She rapped her knuckles on the screen door, then stepped inside.

"Charlie? Are you home?" She walked the short distance through the foyer, then took a single step into the living room.

Charlie was home. He sat in his favorite recliner in the cluttered living room, a handgun on the floor beside him and the pieces of his head decorating the wall in bloody splatters behind him.

Savannah froze, for a moment her mind refused to make sense of the scene before her. In that instant of immobility she was acutely conscious of the pitiful yowls of the dogs coming from the porch, the laughter of a live audience drifting from the television and a mewling noise that she suddenly realized was coming from her.

That moment of blessed denial passed, and the horror struck her like a fist to the stomach. Charlie's sightless blue eyes stared at her as she stumbled backward, fighting the need to be sick, swallowing against the scream that begged to be released.

Tears blurred her vision as she backed out the screen door. She turned blindly, intent on getting to her car, where her cell phone was in her purse on the front seat.

The scream that had been trapped in the back of her throat released itself as a pair of strong hands grabbed her shoulders.

The red-haired, pink-clad woman nearly barreled over Joshua West as he stepped up on the porch of Charlie's house. The shriek she emitted as he caught her by the shoulders nearly shattered his eardrums, but the kick she delivered to his shin sent him backward with a stream of cuss words that would have daunted the devil.

"What in the hell is wrong with you, lady?" he exclaimed as he grabbed the porch rail to steady himself.

She stared up at him, whiskey-colored eyes wide and filled with tears. Her mouth worked, opening and closing, but it was as if the act of speech had left her. Her skin appeared unnaturally pale, a smattering of freckles seeming to stand out a full inch from her cheeks.

As he scowled at her she raised a hand and pointed a trembling finger toward the inside of the house. It was only then that Joshua realized it was fear and horror that rode her features.

He had no idea who she was or what she was doing here, but several other questions quickly filled his head. Why hadn't her ear-splitting scream brought Charlie careening out the door to see what was going on, and why were the dogs running loose?

He took a good, long look at the young woman, in case he had to describe her later, then he went into the house. He'd only taken a single step inside the tiny foyer when he noticed the acrid smell of gunpowder and his gut twisted with a sense of dread.

Smelling gunpowder inside a house was never a good sign. As he took a step into the living room his sense of dread exploded into something deeper, darker. As he stared at Charlie's body, disbelief fought with shock and a quick stab of grief.

It was obvious in a glance that the old man was dead. Joshua was smart enough to know not to disturb anything, although it looked like an open-and-shut case of suicide.

He needed to do something. He needed to call Sheriff Ramsey. Grief threatened to overwhelm the denial, but he shoved it back, knowing there were things that needed to be done.

What had happened here? How on earth had this happened? Dammit, what had made Charlie do such a thing? What had happened to make the man take his own life? Of all the men Joshua had known, he would have thought Charlie the last one who would do something like this.

It was only when he stepped back out of the house that he remembered the woman. She was crouched down next to her car, a hand on Jessie's furry back. As he walked down the steps to the path, she stood, a wary suspicion on her features.

"I called the sheriff," she said, obviously recovering her gift of speech. "He should be here any minute now. Don't come any closer." She held up a can of pepper spray.

Joshua stopped in his tracks. She would have looked quite menacing if the hand holding the spray can weren't shaking so badly.

Some of her color had returned to her face and the freckles now looked as if they belonged on her skin. It was obvious she didn't belong here, didn't belong in Cotter Creek.

She had the sheen of the big city on her, from the toe of her polished boots to the top of her short, curly gelled hair. She represented everything he'd left behind in New York City.

Her hair suited her small, delicate features. She wasn't beautiful, but she was striking. More importantly, there was no blood on her pink sweater or gray cropped slacks. No splatters on the tops of her polished boots.

"Who are you and what are you doing here?" he asked. What had happened in Charlie's house before he'd arrived, and what did she have to do with the old man's death?

"I could ask you the same," she replied, eyes narrowed and finger poised above the sprayer on the can.

"I'm Joshua West and I was just on my way home and decided to stop and say hello to Charlie."

Relief filled her amber-colored eyes and she lowered the can. "I heard they were expecting you either today or tomorrow."

"You didn't answer my questions. Who are you and what in the hell is going on here?" Anger swept through him, much more agreeable than the grief that clawed at his insides as he thought of Charlie.

The relief that had shone from her eyes was short-lived. A frown tugged her thin eyebrows closer together. "My name is Savannah Clarion and I don't know what the hell is going on. I got here about two minutes before you did, just long enough to go inside and find…" She bit her bottom lip as tears welled up.

The anger that had momentarily reared to life dissipated. "Why are you here? Charlie isn't…wasn't exactly the type who liked to entertain guests." And he couldn't imagine that a young woman like her would have an interest in visiting with the old man.

"I was going to interview him. I write a column for the *Cotter Creek Chronicle* called 'People and Personalities.'" Tears spilled onto her cheeks. "Why would he do something like this? I can't believe it."

Joshua raked a hand through his thick, dark hair and frowned. "I just spoke with him two days ago. He seemed fine, his usual self." Judd nuzzled Joshua's hand, seeking a reassuring pat on the head.

"What's going to happen to Judd and Jessie?" Savannah asked. "Who's going to take care of them?"

"I'll take them with me. They'll be well taken care of at Dad's."

"I don't understand this." She wrapped her arms around herself, as if chilled to the bone. "Seems like a drastic way to get out of an interview." She gulped in a deep breath.

He wondered if she was about to get hysterical on him. The last thing he wanted was a hysterical woman on his hands. He shoved his hands in his slacks pockets as he heard the wail of a siren in the distance.

The joyous homecoming he'd expected had transformed into something horrible, and he knew the full realization that Charlie was dead hadn't even struck him yet. What he couldn't yet comprehend was the fact that Charlie hadn't died in his sleep or suffered a heart attack, but, instead, from all indications Charlie had eaten the business end of his gun.

He said no more to Savannah as the sheriff's car pulled onto Charlie's property. *Things have changed,* he thought as he watched Sheriff Jim Ramsey lumber out of his car. The sheriff had put on a bit of weight in the year and a half that Joshua had been gone. His hair was more salt than pepper, and as his gaze fell on Savannah an expression of annoyance flashed on his features. What was that about?

The West family and Sheriff Ramsey had always shared a precarious tolerance for one another. A tolerance that often threatened to dissolve whenever the sheriff felt that the West work stepped on his toes.

Ramsey nodded to Savannah, then walked past her. "Joshua," he greeted with a touch of surprise. "Heard you were expected back here. Hell of a welcome home. Want to tell me what's going on?"

"I was on my way into town and decided to stop and say hello to Charlie. I stepped up on the porch as Ms. Clarion came crashing out the door. I went inside to see Charlie. It looks like he shot himself."

"I came out here to interview him for my column," Savannah said and stepped closer to the two men. "Something isn't right here. Charlie was excited about being interviewed. He would have never done something like this. I want a full investigation into his death."

Ramsey sighed audibly. "I'm going inside. I've already put in a call to Burke McReynolds."

"Burke McReynolds?" Joshua didn't know the name.

"You haven't met him. We hired him on a month ago as a part-time medical examiner. If I have any more questions for the two of you, I know where to find you both. There's no reason for you to hang around here."

It was an obvious dismissal, and Joshua was more than ready to leave this place of death. There was nothing he could do for Charlie, and more than anything he was eager to get home to his family.

"I'm not going anywhere," Savannah replied. Although her eyes still shone with tears, she raised her chin and looked at the sheriff defiantly. "I have a responsibility to my readers, a responsibility to Charlie."

The annoyance that had flashed momentarily across Ramsey's features appeared again. "Savannah, you write a gossip column and there's nothing you can do for Charlie. Now you go on and get out of here. We don't need you in the way as we go about our business."

If her face had lacked color before, it didn't now. A flush of red swept up her slender neck and took over her face, nearly matching the bright red of her hair.

"There's something rotten in this town, Sheriff Ramsey, and I'm not going to quit until I figure out what it is." She stomped to her car and got inside.

"What was that all about?" Joshua asked Ramsey as she pealed out and took off down the road.

"Who knows. Just spare me from Lois Lane wannabes." Jim sighed again. "I got work to do." As he headed for Charlie's front door, Joshua loaded Jessie and Judd into the backseat of his car, then got in behind the steering wheel.

As Ramsey disappeared into the house, Joshua

thought of Savannah Clarion's parting words. *"Something was rotten in Cotter Creek."*

What was she talking about? What in the hell had happened in his town in the time that he'd been gone?

Chapter 2

Savannah awakened with grief pressing thickly against her chest. The early-morning October sunshine drifted through the frilly lace curtains in her bedroom, and all she wanted to do was pull the pillow over her head and forget what had happened the day before.

Charlie was dead. The thought hit her in the stomach with the force of a blow. Other than Meredith and her landlady, Winnie, Charlie had been the only friend she'd made since coming to town. And now he was gone, dead in a way that made no sense whatsoever.

She'd never again see that slow, easy grin of his, never hear his acerbic sense of humor or match her wits against his in a game of chess.

"Charlie," she whispered, her voice nothing more than a hollow echo of itself.

She wanted to weep, but she'd spent most of her tears the night before. Besides, crying didn't change anything and neither did covering her face with a pillow and hiding in bed all day. She owed Charlie more than tears, more than denial.

She was a reporter, and even though her published work so far was nothing more than a couple of gossip columns and fluff pieces, as Sheriff Ramsey had characterized them, it was time she became an investigative reporter and found out the truth about what had happened to Charlie. She owed the old man that much.

Galvanized with a new determination, she showered, then dressed in a pair of black pencil-thin slacks and a lightweight lavender sweater. Even though it was only the first week of October, the weather had been unusually cool.

The scent of bacon and freshly brewed coffee greeted her as she stepped out of her room and headed downstairs. No matter what time Savannah got up in the morning, her elderly landlady was always up before her.

Winnie sat at the kitchen table, a cup of coffee in front of her. She smiled a greeting as Savannah entered the kitchen. "Coffee's on and the bacon is fried. All you need to tell me is how many eggs you want."

"None. I'm not hungry this morning." Savannah went to the cabinet that held the coffee mugs, then poured herself a cup of the brew and joined Winnie at the table.

She suspected the old woman hadn't rented the upstairs of her house to Savannah because she needed the money but rather because she wanted companionship and somebody to cook for. Winnie's husband had died three years before, and it was obvious she was lonely.

"How did you sleep?" Winnie asked, the wrinkles in her forehead deepening in concern. When Savannah had come home from Charlie's place the day before she'd told Winnie what had happened.

Savannah wrapped her hands around the warm coffee mug in an attempt to fight off a chill. "Terrible." She suddenly remembered the nightmares that had plagued her all night, visions of blood and death and poor Charlie.

Winnie shook her head. "I just don't understand it. I don't understand how anyone becomes so desperate they commit suicide." She paused a moment to take a sip of her coffee. "Why, I saw Charlie yesterday at the grocery store and he seemed just fine."

Savannah stared at Winnie. "You saw Charlie at the grocery store? What time?"

"I don't know, it must have been around noon. We met in the ice cream section and he told me how much he loves butter pecan and I told him I was quite partial to plain old chocolate."

"Did he buy ice cream?"

Winnie frowned. "I saw him get a gallon out of

the freezer, but I didn't see him when he left the store."

Savannah took a sip of her coffee, her brain burning up as it worked overtime. She knew how much Charlie had loved his butter pecan ice cream. Many evenings she'd shared a bowl with him as they had played a game of chess.

Did a man who planned to commit suicide buy groceries? Did a man who intended to take his own life buy a gallon of ice cream?

All through the night her gut instinct had told her that Charlie didn't commit suicide, and the fact that the old man had bought ice cream an hour or so before his death only deepened her gut instinct.

Winnie eyed her over the rim of her coffee cup. Despite being seventy-two years old, Winnie was still a sharp tack. "What's going on in that head of yours, Savannah?"

"I just don't believe that Charlie committed suicide. Aside from the fact that he bought ice cream a short time before his death, I know Charlie would have never done something like that, knowing I was coming to his house. He would have never wanted me to find him like that."

"Then what do you think happened?"

"I think Charlie was murdered. He was murdered and somebody made it look like a suicide and I intend to prove it."

"How are you going to do that?"

Savannah frowned thoughtfully. "I'm not sure.

One of the first things I need to do is talk to Sheriff Ramsey." She took a sip of her coffee, then shook her head. "There's been too many deaths around here lately." Strange falls off tractors and from haylofts, a gas heater explosion and other odd deaths. The citizens of Cotter Creek were either unusually unlucky or something more frightening was going on.

She suddenly thought of the handsome hunk she'd literally bumped into on Charlie's porch the night before. "What do you know about Joshua West?"

A smile curved Winnie's lips. "Before he left town I think every rancher in the area was locking up their daughters for safekeeping. He's a charmer, spoiled as a dozen eggs left out in the sun too long, but like all those West boys he's got a good heart."

Savannah didn't care if he was a charmer, or spoiled or had a good heart. His attraction as far as she was concerned was that he was a local who had been out of town for a while and might have some objectivity that could work to her advantage.

But, more importantly, she knew the West name carried weight in Cotter Creek and the sheriff would give more credence to Joshua than he ever would to her. She had a feeling if she wanted people to take her seriously about Charlie's death, then it wouldn't hurt to have Joshua West on her side.

"Are you sure you don't want something for breakfast?" Winnie asked. "You know a good breakfast is always the way to start a good day."

Savannah laughed. "My mother believed a protein shake and an hour on a StairMaster was the way to start each day."

"That's what happens to people when they got more money than sense," Winnie scoffed. "A couple of eggs?"

Savannah relented and nodded her head. She suspected Winnie didn't care so much about what she ate but wasn't quite ready for Savannah to fly out the door and leave her alone for the day.

It was after nine when Savannah left the house, her stomach full and a renewed burn of determination in her soul. Her first stop was at the sheriff's office, where she was disappointed to learn that Sheriff Ramsey wasn't in.

She left the office, got into her car and headed for the West ranch. She hoped she could enlist Joshua West's help in demanding a full investigation into Charlie's death. Charlie deserved at least that much, and, as far as Savannah was concerned, Sheriff Ramsey hadn't been too diligent in following up on other deaths in the small town.

The West ranch was a sprawl of pasture surrounding a huge rambling home with a long wooden porch that was perfect for sitting and watching the sunset in the evenings. On more than one occasion in the last couple of months she and Meredith had sat on the porch, talking while the sun went down.

Savannah had always found friendships difficult.

From the time she was young her mother had chosen her friends. They had to be beautiful, stylish and from privileged backgrounds. Savannah had never fit in and had found it difficult to trust females so different than her.

But Meredith West was another story. She certainly came from a family who had tons of money, but she suffered no airs, didn't judge people by their clothes or their looks. She was refreshingly normal after Savannah's years of being surrounded by superficiality.

It was Meredith who answered Savannah's knock. As usual the tall brunette was clad in a pair of jeans and a sweatshirt. Her long dark hair was in a careless ponytail. "Savannah." She opened the screen door, stepped out on the porch and drew Savannah into the warmth of an embrace. "I heard about Charlie. I'm so sorry."

A wave of grief swept over Savannah, but she shoved it aside. She had no time for grief. She was on a mission. "Thanks, I still can't believe it myself."

"I was going to call you this morning to see how you were doing."

"I'm doing okay. Actually, I'm here to see your brother."

Meredith frowned. "My brother? Which one?"

"Joshua. Is he home?"

"He's here, but he's out riding at the moment. Come on in. He should be back before too long." Meredith ushered her into the house and toward the kitchen.

Smokey Johnson, the West cook and the man who had helped raise the West children when their mother had been murdered, scowled as the two women entered the room he considered his exclusive domain.

"You be nice, Smokey," Meredith exclaimed. "Savannah is quite fragile this morning."

The old man snorted. "Red-haired girls aren't fragile. They're tough as nails, got to be to get through all the teasing they take when they're young."

Savannah was accustomed to Smokey, who was a cliché of a tough old coot with a heart of gold. "I'm not feeling fragile this morning. I'm feeling more than a little pissed off because I think somebody killed my friend and made it look like a suicide."

Smokey pointed a gnarled finger toward a chair at the table. "What are you talking about? According to what Joshua told us when he got home last night it was an open-and-shut case of suicide."

Meredith gazed at Savannah sympathetically. "Everyone knew how much Charlie missed his wife since her death eight years ago. Maybe he just got tired of waiting to join her in the hereafter."

Savannah shook her head vehemently. "After eight years? Give me a break. Sure, Charlie missed Rebecca and he was looking forward to the time when they would be together again, but he also believed that everyone went when it was time for them to go. After eight years of being alone why would he suddenly decide to end it all?"

Before anyone could reply, the back door opened and Joshua stepped into the kitchen. He stopped short at the sight of her and frowned. "What in the hell are you doing here?"

"Joshua!" Meredith shot her brother a dirty look. "Where are your manners?"

"I lost them when she kicked me in the shin hard enough to half cripple me yesterday."

Warmth swept up Savannah's neck as she remembered the kick she'd delivered to him. "I thought you'd killed Charlie."

She'd recognized in the brief time she'd seen him the day before that he was handsome, but his attractiveness today hit her like a kick from a horse.

She hadn't noticed yesterday just how thick and shiny his dark hair was, or the amazing green of his eyes. She hadn't paid attention to his raw masculinity that today screamed from him.

Clad in a pair of jeans and a long-sleeved knit shirt that pulled tautly across broad shoulders and a flat stomach, he was blatantly male and sexy as hell.

Winnie had said he was a charmer, but there was nothing charming in the look he shot her. He looked irritated and tense and just a whisper away from dangerous.

"If you'll excuse me, I'm heading to the shower," he said.

Savannah popped out of the chair. "Actually, I'm here to talk to you. Would it be possible for us to speak somewhere alone?"

"I can't imagine what we'd have to talk about." He started out of the kitchen and with a glance of apology to Meredith and Smokey, Savannah followed Joshua.

"Of course we have things to talk about," she exclaimed, unable to help but notice that he had a perfect butt for jeans. "We were both at a crime scene. We should compare notes and see if we can help the investigation."

His long strides carried him down the hallway toward the master bathroom. "There's no notes to compare. The investigation is over. I spoke to Ramsey early this morning, and according to him there's no reason not to think it's anything but a suicide."

"Ramsey is an overweight, lazy, incompetent jerk who is just biding time until his retirement at the end of the year," she protested.

She jumped in surprise and stumbled a step backward as he unexpectedly twisted around to face her in the bathroom doorway.

"And he told me you were an overeager, conspiracy theorist who was desperate to find a story that will take you away from writing silly gossip columns and gain you some real respect." He yanked his shirt over his head and threw it to the bathroom floor behind him.

Savannah tried to maintain focus as she was presented a broad, bare, muscled chest that would make most women weak in the knees. "That's not true.

Ramsey doesn't like me because I'm questioning his investigation skills."

Joshua's hands went to the waist of his jeans where they unfastened the first button on his fly. A lazy smile curved his lips upward. For just a moment there didn't seem to be enough oxygen in the area.

"Unless you want to discuss this while I scrub your back, I suggest you take a hike," he said.

For just a brief, insane moment the idea of this sexy man washing her back was infinitely appealing. But she reminded herself why she was here and why it was important to get Joshua West on her side.

"All right, I'll take a hike right now, but sooner or later you need to hear what I have to tell you. Something isn't right in this town, and somebody needs to do something about it." Hoping she sounded mysterious enough to pique his interest, she turned on her heel and stomped back to the kitchen.

Joshua walked toward the white tent that had been set up in the cemetery for Charlie Summit's funeral. When he'd parked, he'd been dismayed to see so few cars here. It appeared that Charlie was going to go out of this world much like he'd spent most of the past eight years of his life…alone.

Joshua knew all about feeling alone, although in the year and a half he'd spent in New York City, he'd rarely been alone.

He'd worked hard and had played even harder. He'd thrown himself into the Manhattan single lifestyle, serial-dating sharp, beautiful women with fascinating careers. But in spite of all that he'd never shaken a core sense of homesickness that had eaten at him day and night.

Failure. A little voice whispered in his head. He'd struck out on his own, determined to make a life separate from his family. He'd wanted to be his own man, but in the end he'd run back home like a wounded puppy.

Although he had been successful as a stockbroker, the shambles of his personal life had finally forced him to get out of town and head back to Cotter Creek.

His father, Red West, had just assumed Joshua would step back into the family business and work for Wild West Protection Services as a bodyguard, but Joshua had told his dad he was taking a little time off to decide what he wanted to do. Going to work for the family business felt like yet another failure.

He shoved these thoughts aside as he approached the tent, the scent of too-sweet flowers cloying in the air. Charlie had left a will with an account set up for his funeral. He'd wanted only a gravesite service and to be buried beside his beloved wife, Rebecca. Together in life, now together again in death.

As he entered the white structure, he stiffened at the sight of Savannah Clarion. She stood next to Winnie Halifax, Savannah's hair sparkling and appearing even more red against the black of her long-sleeved blouse and black slacks.

He nodded to the preacher, then took up a position

on the opposite side of the casket from Savannah, who had been an irritating pain in his ass over the past three days.

She'd left a message at the house every day, requesting that he call her back, but the last thing Joshua wanted was to get mixed up in any drama. He'd had enough of that before he'd left New York.

Within a few minutes others began to arrive. His sister, Meredith appeared with his dad and Smokey. Meredith hurried to Savannah's side, while his father and Smokey joined him.

Raymond Buchannan, the owner of the Cotter Creek newspaper, arrived, looking old and tired. Joshua realized the man must be close to eighty and wondered if he ever intended to retire.

Mayor Aaron Sharp also arrived, shaking everyone's hands as if he were at a political campaign instead of a funeral.

Finally the service began. As Reverend Baxter talked about life and death and redemption, Joshua found himself looking again and again at Savannah.

He hadn't thought her particularly pretty the day he'd seen her at Charlie's house, but there was something in her irregular features that was arresting.

The dark red curls suited her, complemented by her eyes, which were a mix of gold and copper. She had a killer figure, slender hips and long legs and was unusually busty for a slim woman.

Over the past three days Meredith had made it her job to extol the virtues of her friend to him. Witty and smart. Fun-loving and soft-hearted. Tenacious and outspoken. He'd heard more about Savannah Clarion than he'd ever wanted to know.

He had a feeling his sister was attempting to indulge in a little matchmaking, but Meredith didn't realize the last thing Joshua wanted in his life was any kind of a relationship with a woman.

Unlike his brothers, who seemed to have a knack when it came to the opposite sex, Joshua had failed miserably in that respect as well.

Grief for Charlie shoved every other thought out of his head. The old man had been a special friend to Joshua before he'd left Cotter Creek, and Joshua would miss him.

He was grateful when the service ended. He didn't hang around to make nice with the other funeral attendees, but rather slipped out of the tent the minute the service was complete.

Instead of walking to where his car was parked, he followed the path to another area of the cemetery, the place where his mother was buried.

The entire right corner of the cemetery contained the West plots. His mother was buried beneath a grand red maple tree whose leaves were just beginning to turn scarlet with autumn grandeur.

He stood before her headstone. Elizabeth West, beloved wife, beloved mother. Joshua had never known her. He'd been a baby when she'd gone to the grocery store one evening and later had been found dead beside her car on the side of the road. She'd been strangled, and her murderer had never been found.

Sometimes Joshua wondered what his life would have been like if he'd had a mother, if he'd been raised by a woman instead of by his father and the cantankerous Smokey, who had run the house like an army barrack.

He'd heard stories about his mother, a beautiful woman who had given up an acting career to marry his father and build a family here in Cotter Creek. But he knew her only from photos and didn't have a single memory of his own.

"Meredith told me about your mother's death."

Joshua stiffened at the sound of Savannah's voice. The woman was as tenacious as an Oklahoma tick on the back of a hound dog. He turned around to look at her, noting how the sunshine sparked in her hair. "What do you want from me?"

"I want you to listen to me, that's all. Just hear me out with an open mind. Did you know that Charlie went grocery shopping an hour before his death? Did you know that he bought a gallon of butter pecan ice cream? Why does a man who is suicidal buy groceries that nobody will eat?"

She talked fast, as if afraid she wouldn't get everything out before he walked away from her. "Joshua, Charlie knew I was coming to interview him. He would have never killed himself knowing that I was expected to be there, that I would be the one to find him like that. Charlie would have never done that to me."

As much as Joshua didn't want to get caught up in what he'd considered her drama, her words gave him pause. "Maybe he went shopping then got depressed. Maybe he wasn't suicidal until five minutes before he picked up his gun."

She shook her head, red curls bouncing. "At least three times a week I spent the evenings with Charlie. I'm telling you the man wasn't depressed. He wasn't suicidal. He had plans, big plans. He was going to plant a flower garden next spring, fill it with all the flowers his wife had loved. He was thinking about taking lessons to learn how to play bridge."

Joshua wished he had touched base with Charlie more often while he'd been in New York. He'd called every couple of weeks, but the calls had been brief, too brief.

"It's not just Charlie," Savannah continued. "There have been others deaths…too many."

He suddenly remembered her parting words to Ramsey the day of Charlie's death, that something was rotten in Cotter Creek and she intended to get to the bottom of it. "What deaths? What are you talking about?"

She glanced around, then looked back at him. "It's too complicated to go over all of it now."

"Why me? Why are you coming to me with all this?"

She frowned, the gesture wrinkling her freckled nose with charming appeal. "For two reasons. First of all you've been out of town for a while. I figure you'll be more objective about things than any of the other locals. Secondly, you're a West and that holds a lot of weight in this area of the country."

"Meredith is a West, why not enlist her help?" he countered. He tried not to notice her scent, a spicy musk that was intensely pleasant.

"I told you the other day that Sheriff Ramsey was lazy and incompetent. The man is also a raging sexist. He wouldn't pay any more attention to Meredith than he has to me."

Despite his reluctance to the contrary, he was intrigued. "Okay, I'm listening," he said.

She glanced over her shoulder to where Winnie stood in the distance, obviously waiting for her. "I can't go into it all now. Besides, I have some research at the newspaper office. I'd like you to see it."

He had a feeling she wasn't going to stop bothering him until he agreed at least to see what she thought she had. "Okay, just tell me when and where to meet you and I'll see what you've got."

Her features lit with relief. "We need to meet at the newspaper office, but I'd rather do it when Mr. Buchannan isn't there. He always leaves the office at around eight in the evenings. Could you meet me there tonight about nine?"

Somewhere deep inside him, he knew this was probably a mistake. But, since returning to Cotter Creek, he'd felt unsettled. He'd grown accustomed to the fast pace of the city, of having places to go and things to do. In truth, he was bored, and he told himself that was the only reason he was agreeing to meet her.

"All right, nine tonight at the newspaper office," he said.

She smiled. The look softened her features and transformed her from arresting into something close to beautiful. "I'll see you tonight. And Joshua, thanks." She turned and hurried toward Winnie.

Joshua stared after her, wishing he could take back his agreement to meet her. He had a feeling he'd made yet another mistake in a long string of mistakes that had been made in the past year and a half.

Chapter 3

The *Cotter Creek Chronicle* office was located on the bottom floor of a two-story brick building on Main Street. The front of the building was a large picture window, at the moment as dark as the night that surrounded Savannah as she parked her car in front.

It was eight-forty-five, and Main Street was completely deserted. Most of the shops and businesses closed their doors at eight-thirty. The only nightlife Cotter Creek had to offer was a couple of taverns on the edge of town.

She turned off her car engine and tapped a pale pink fingernail on her steering wheel, a surge of excitement filling her.

Finally, finally she had somebody who would

listen to her. She certainly hadn't been able to get her boss, Raymond Buchannan, interested in her theories. All he wanted from her were fluff pieces that would please a more feminine audience.

"I write the news fit to print," he'd told her the last time she'd broached him about the multitude of deaths in the Cotter Creek area. "I reported what happened in each of those deaths, and there's nothing left to report."

Nor had Sheriff Ramsey or Mayor Aaron Sharp been interested in what she'd had to say. This town definitely had a good old boy network and she had several strikes against her. First, she was a woman. Second, she was an outsider. And last, she had a feeling that most everyone in town thought she was here only to make a name for herself and have a body of work to take to a bigger newspaper job.

Nothing could be further from the truth. It had taken her only a week in this dusty Oklahoma town to fall in love with Cotter Creek. She had no intention of going anywhere. In fact, she had broached the topic of buying the paper from Raymond Buchannan when he decided to retire. If he ever decided to retire.

She had enough money in a savings account to be able to meet whatever price Buchannan settled on when he did decide to sell. Thankfully her parents had begun investing for her when she was a baby, and on her twenty-first birthday those funds had become available to her. Over the past four years she'd tried not to touch that money unless it was absolutely necessary, believing that it was her nest egg for the future.

At exactly nine o'clock a big black pickup pulled into the parking space next to hers. Joshua got out of the vehicle, and Savannah tried not to notice his physical attractiveness.

He was clad in a pair of black slacks, a black turtleneck and a worn leather bomber jacket. His hair was slightly tousled, as if he'd driven with the window down and the night breeze had blown through his dark locks.

The last thing she was looking for was to be attracted to any man, but especially one who had the reputation for being a player, at least before he'd left town. Besides, men who looked like Joshua West didn't date women who looked like her, and she'd do well to remember that.

She quickly got out of her car and smiled at him. "Thanks for coming. I really appreciate it."

He gave her a curt nod, his expression letting her know he would rather be anywhere but here at the moment. She pulled her keys from her purse and walked to the front door of the newspaper office.

"All I ask of you is to please keep an open mind when I show you everything I've compiled. It took a while and a lot of research before I finally started to make some horrifying connections." She was rambling. When she was nervous she always rambled and something about the silent man standing next to her made her nervous.

She sighed in relief as she got the door open. She stepped inside, flipped on the overhead lights, then walked across the wooden floor toward a small room in the back that served as her office.

She was conscious of Joshua close behind her, his loafers ringing on the floor. He had yet to say a word, and that only made her anxiety increase.

If he saw the material she'd gathered and judged her as some crazy conspiracy theorist looking for a story she didn't know what she'd do. She hadn't felt so right about anything since she'd been seventeen years old and told her mother that she absolutely, positively was not getting a breast reduction.

The office Buchannan had given her to work in was little more than the size of a storage closet. It was only large enough to contain her desk and office chair. She'd tried to dress up the small space, claim it as her own by placing things she liked on the scarred wooden desk.

There was a basket of her favorite candy bars, a stuffed frog that one of her friends had given her for luck when she'd left Scottsdale and, finally, there was a plaque that read, Live Well, Laugh Hard.

Joshua picked up one of the candy bars and gave her a wry look. "Guess you aren't into counting calories."

"Never," she replied and punched the button to boot up her computer. "My mother started counting my calories the day I was born. When I finally got out on my own I decided I was going to eat whatever the heck I wanted."

He nodded, a touch of amusement lightening his green eyes. "That's one of the things that drove me crazy about the women in New York. None of them eat. I'd take a lady out to dinner and it would have been just as easy to toss her a head of lettuce and call it a night."

Despite her nervous tension, Savannah laughed. "You take me out to dinner and I'll eat your money's worth," she exclaimed, then hurriedly added, "not that I think you'd ever take me out to dinner. I mean, not that I'd even want you to take me to dinner."

His amusement was even more evident as he simply stood there and watched as she dug a hole with her tongue. She flushed and bit her lip to stop her mouth from running away with her.

Thankfully at that moment the computer loaded up and she sat in the chair in front of it to retrieve the files she wanted him to see.

He moved behind her and she was intensely aware of his nearness. He smelled like the outdoors, a scent of fresh Oklahoma sunshine and night breeze and beneath that a clean cologne that tantalized her senses.

"I started all this because of what happened to Kate Sampson's father," she said as she finally found the file she wanted and opened it.

Kate Sampson's father, Gray, had been murdered three months before. It had been Joshua's brother Zack who had ridden to her rescue and helped her solve the murder. But the one thing the investigation hadn't yielded was a credible motive for his murder.

"I think maybe Zack's planning on running for

sheriff in November," Joshua said, his breath warm on the nape of her neck.

"I'm sure he'll do a far better job than Ramsey," she replied and hit the print button. "You might not know it, but Gray Sampson was killed by a ranch hand named Sonny Williams."

"I heard. My brother Clay told me about Gray's murder and Sonny's arrest."

She pulled up another file and began the print process, then turned around in the chair to face him. "But, did you know that Sonny Williams supposedly killed himself in jail? Did you know that before he died he said that Gray's death was just a part of a bigger plan?"

Joshua frowned. "I might have been told something about that, but I was a thousand miles away and to be honest had other things on my mind."

"Gray Sampson's death wasn't the beginning of things." She stood and grabbed the material from the printer. "Let's go back out to Raymond's desk."

The space in her office was too small for the two of them as far as she was concerned. Joshua was too tall, too male to share such a tiny space with her.

She breathed a sigh of relief as they returned to the main office area. At least in here she could breathe without smelling the scent of him.

She sat at Raymond's desk and motioned him into the chair on the opposite side of the desk. "Are you a wannabe true crime writer or what?" he asked.

The question irritated her. He knew nothing about

her but was already making judgments. "No, I'm not. When I took the job here I decided it was a good idea to read as many of the back issues of the paper as possible to familiarize myself with both the newspaper I'd be writing for and the town where I'd chosen to live."

"And why did you choose Cotter Creek?" His green gaze held hers intently, as if he were seeking answers to questions he hadn't yet spoken.

"To be perfectly honest, I feel as if Cotter Creek chose me." She broke eye contact with him, finding his direct gaze somewhat disconcerting. Instead she looked at the framed front page of the first copy of the *Cotter Creek Chronicle* that hung on the wall just behind him.

"I wasn't sure where I was going when I left Scottsdale and eventually made it to Cotter Creek where my car transmission blew. It took a couple of days to fix and, while I was waiting, I just fell in love with the town."

"And how did you meet Charlie?"

She looked at him again, fighting a wave of impatience. "I thought you were here to see the material I have, not to play a game of twenty questions."

He smiled, one that lifted only a corner of his mouth with sexy laziness. "I like to know a little bit about the people I deal with."

"Fine. I'm twenty-four years old. I love animals and candy bars, I hate superficiality and people who don't have a sense of humor."

She leaned forward, meeting his gaze directly. "I met Charlie on the first day I arrived in town. I'd just left my car at Mechanic's Mansion and was looking for a hotel or motel to stay in while the car was being fixed. There were a couple of teenagers on the corner and I asked them about accommodations, and they told me there was a nice bed-and-breakfast on the edge of town."

His eyes began to glitter with humor, obviously seeing where her story was leading. "Anyway," she continued, "one of the boys offered to drive me there. He took me to the entrance to Charlie's place and left me there."

"I'll bet you were horrified," he said.

She laughed. "When I broke through the trees and saw Charlie's place, I suspected I'd been had, but I wasn't one hundred percent sure so I marched up to Charlie's door and told him I'd heard he ran the best bed and breakfast in town."

She smiled at the memory of Charlie's face and a swift sharp grief pierced through her, stealing her smile and forcing the sting of tears to her eyes. She raised a hand to swipe them away.

"Sorry, I didn't mean to upset you." His voice was gentle and she saw real regret in his eyes.

She nodded. "I'm just going to miss him so much. Other than your sister and Winnie, Charlie was my only friend in town. We used to spend hours playing chess." She released a small laugh. "I never got a chance to beat him."

"I could never beat him either." For a long moment their gazes remained locked. It was a moment of connection, two people mourning for somebody they had both loved. This time he broke the eye contact and gestured to the papers in front of her. "Okay, show me what you've got."

She cleared her throat, stuffing her emotions for Charlie back deep inside. "I noticed when I was reading back issues of the paper that there seemed to be an unusual number of fatal accidents in the area."

"It's a ranching and farming community, there are always accidents."

"True, but Cotter Creek seemed to have more than its share, so two weeks ago I did some statistical analysis, comparing like-size ranching and farming communities. What I discovered was that the incidence of accidental deaths was three hundred times higher in Cotter Creek than anywhere else I compared it with."

Joshua raised a dark eyebrow and took the sheet of paper that held her data. She watched him as he studied it. She'd met most of his brothers, each more handsome than the next, but Joshua seemed to have gotten the West good-looking gene in spades.

Savannah had been raised among the beautiful people of Scottsdale and if they weren't beautiful by nature, then plastic surgery solved the problem. She'd been the anomaly, a busty redhead with a snub nose covered in freckles, who had no interest in bee-stung lips or liposuction.

By nature she didn't particularly trust handsome men. She knew she was the kind of girl handsome men took home only when all the pretty blondes and brunettes had left the party.

She'd had one relationship with a man who'd been so attractive he'd taken her breath away, but it had turned out to be a cliché. He'd left her for a gorgeous woman who had taken his breath away.

But she needed to trust Joshua West. She needed him in her corner.

Her mind flashed with an image of him standing in the bathroom doorway, his chest splendidly naked and tautly muscled. A wave of warmth fluttered through her at the memory. Her last relationship had been almost a year ago, long enough that she'd almost forgotten what it felt like to have a warm naked chest pressed against her own. Almost…but not quite.

"Okay." He set the paper back on the desk and looked at her, no trace of humor in his gaze. "You've got my attention."

"Trust me, that's just the beginning," she said. She handed him the next paper she'd printed off. "This is a list of all the deaths that have occurred in Cotter Creek in the past two years." She focused on her subject and tried to forget the vision of his naked chest that had popped unbidden into her head.

"If you take each one separately, they don't seem so ominous…a tractor accident, a fall from a hayloft, a gas heater malfunction. You know Gray Sampson's death had initially been ruled accidental. Sheriff

Ramsey assumed he'd been thrown from his horse and had hit his head on a rock."

She talked faster and faster, needing to get everything out. "It was only when Gray's daughter and your brother Zack began to investigate that they realized it wasn't an accident, but instead was murder."

Joshua held up a hand to stop her. "Take a breath before you pass out."

She felt a blush sweep up her neck. "Sorry, I've just been waiting so long for somebody to really listen to me. For the last week and a half I've been telling anyone and everyone that something isn't right here, but nobody is interested in hearing me out."

"Right now all you've convinced me of is that in the past year and a half the people of Cotter Creek were either more careless or more unlucky than others."

"I'm not finished yet," she replied. "By the time I am, you'll see that something terrible is happening in this town, and unless somebody does something about it, more people are going to die."

Joshua had yet to make up his mind about Savannah. He wasn't sure if she was a drama queen looking for excitement or was really onto something.

She'd surprised him with her statistical analysis and the sharp intelligence that gleamed from her amber-colored eyes.

The one thing he did know was that something

about Savannah Clarion made him a little bit jumpy, made his thoughts race in directions they shouldn't be going.

As she'd talked to him, he'd found himself wondering if her red curls were soft and silky or wiry and coarse. He'd wondered if her full mouth would be soft and yielding beneath his or fierce and demanding?

Those kinds of thoughts irritated him. Hadn't he learned his lesson in New York? He focused his attention on the next piece of paper she shoved over in front of him.

"I made a list of all the people who have died. As you can see, all of them are men," she said.

He read the list of names, then looked back at her. "Look, this is all very interesting, but I don't see any big conspiracy here."

She frowned, her lower lip jutting out slightly in what appeared to be a small pout. "I'm not finished with all the investigating I intend to do," she said. "Help me, Joshua. Please help me find out exactly what happened to all these men. With two of us working together it will take half the time to get some answers."

He leaned back in his chair and swiped a hand through his hair. "I'm not sure what the questions are that need to be asked."

"We need to look at each individual incident and see if there are any anomalies, anything that doesn't fit with it being an accident. Like I said before, Gray Sampson's death would have been ruled an accident.

It wasn't until your brother picked up the rock where Gray had supposedly fallen off his horse and hit his head and saw blood on both sides that they realized the rock had been used to bludgeon him to death."

She paused to draw a deep breath and he tried not to notice the rise and fall of her breasts beneath the light lavender sweater she wore.

"As far as I'm concerned, Charlie buying ice cream an hour before he supposedly committed suicide is a huge red flag," she continued. "Joshua, you were his friend. You should know Charlie didn't have a suicidal bone in his body. Don't you want to know the truth? Isn't Charlie worth a little of your time?"

Joshua sighed. He had to admit that the fact that Charlie bought groceries then went home and blew his brains out, didn't make sense. Charlie's wife Rebecca had been gone a long time and Charlie seemed to have made peace with the fact that he would live out the rest of his years alone.

Surely if a man was going to commit suicide to be with his departed wife, he wouldn't wait eight long years. Charlie's suicide just didn't make sense, although any other scenario didn't make sense either.

What else do you have to do with your time, a little voice whispered inside his head? He didn't want to work the family business and he wasn't interested in continuing as a stockbroker, but had no idea what he really wanted to do. He had nothing but time on his hands at the moment.

"All right," he relented after a moment's hesitation. "I'll do some checking into these deaths. I'll get the accident reports and look them over."

"Thank you." She smiled and he felt a jolt of heat sweep through him. She had one hell of a smile. She grabbed a sheet of paper and scribbled something then handed it to him. "That's my phone number at Winnie's and my cell phone number."

He took them reluctantly, having no intention of calling her except to tell her he'd done as she'd requested. Something about her unsettled him and the less interaction she had with him the better he'd feel. "It should just take me a day or two." He stood, eager to be away from her with her sexy scent and heart-stopping smile.

She handed him the papers she'd printed off and he folded them and stuck them in his back pocket. "Why did you decide to come back to Cotter Creek?" she asked, also rising. "Meredith told me you'd been doing quite well in New York."

I ran back home like a dog with my tail tucked between my legs. I screwed up with a relationship that turned more than ugly. The thoughts flew through his head, bringing with him the sense of failure that had ridden his shoulders since he'd made the decision to return home.

"I missed my family. When you're used to being surrounded by people who care about you, a place like New York City can be pretty lonely."

She eyed him wryly. "I doubt if a man like you had too many lonely nights."

"There's a difference between being alone and being lonely." He gestured toward the door, uncomfortable with the personal turn of the conversation.

"Must be nice to have a loving family," she said as she gathered her papers, then joined him at the front door.

"You aren't close with your family?" he asked. She stood close enough to him that he could again smell her scent, a heady fragrance that put all his nerves on alert.

"It's just me and my parents," she replied. "I don't think my mother ever recovered from the shock of not birthing a perfect blond, beautiful miniature of herself, and my father was mostly absent while I was growing up. He had to work long hours to keep my mother in baubles and bling."

She turned out the light, locked the door and they stepped out of the building. Night had completely fallen, but the illumination from a full moon cascaded down, painting her features in a soft, becoming light.

"I can't thank you enough for meeting me here tonight and listening to me."

"Don't thank me yet," he warned. "You haven't convinced me that there's anything ominous going on."

She nodded, her curls dancing with the gesture. "How are Jessie and Judd?"

Joshua thought of the two dogs he'd brought home from Charlie's place. "Initially they were confused and seemed depressed, but they're beginning to settle in just fine. Smokey wasn't thrilled that I'd brought them home."

She laughed, a low throaty sound. "Is that man ever happy about anything?"

He grinned. "Smokey's bark is definitely louder than his bite. After my mother's death I'm not sure my father could have coped with six small children without Smokey's help."

"How did that happen? I mean, where did he come from?"

"Smokey worked as a foreman on the ranch until a terrible fall from a horse crushed his leg and left him with permanent damage. He'd just about healed from his wounds when my mother was murdered. Smokey stepped into the house as if he were born to the job."

"I'd love to interview him for my column. Actually, I'd love to interview you, you know, something about the return of the prodigal son."

"No way, I'm not interested in being interviewed. And good luck with Smokey," he added drily. At that moment a loud bang resounded and almost simultaneously the picture window just to the right of them exploded.

Without thought, acting only on instinct, Joshua dove toward Savannah and tackled her to the ground.

Chapter 4

Savannah hit the pavement hard, the back of her head connecting with the concrete with a dull whack that momentarily created whirling stars in her brain. Joshua's body covered hers as shards of glass rained down around them.

For a moment she was frozen, unable to think. The back of her head throbbed from the blow. She opened her eyes and winced. "What happened?" she asked as the initial shock began to wear off.

"Shh." He shushed her sharply. She could swear she felt his heart pounding against her chest, but then wasn't sure if it was his or her own beating so frantically.

In the moonlight she could see his features, taut

and dangerous-looking as he gazed at the darkness across the street.

What was he looking for? What had just happened? A dog barked in the distance, the only sound in the otherwise silent night. "What's going on? Do you see anything?" she whispered.

"Where are your keys to the office?" His voice was like hers, just a whisper.

She dug her hand into her pocket and withdrew the keys. He took them from her. For the first time since they'd fallen to the pavement, he looked down at her. "I'm going to open the office door and when I do, I want you to crawl inside. Whatever you do, don't stand up."

His eyes gleamed more silver than green in the moonlight. Dangerous. He looked so dangerous it frightened her. "What happened, Joshua?" she asked again, her fear evident in her voice. "What's going on?"

"Somebody just took a shot at us." His eyes narrowed as he once again looked across the street. "And I don't know if the shooter is still there waiting for us to make a move or not."

A shot? Somebody had shot at them? Fear swelled inside her. Her head throbbed with nauseating intensity. "I told you something was rotten in this town." Her voice rose in volume. Surely this was proof. "I must be onto something and now somebody is trying to shut me up."

"How about you shut up right now until we get inside and can call the sheriff."

She would have been offended by his words if she hadn't been so busy trying to process the fact that apparently somebody had just tried to kill them.

As he started to get off her, she had the crazy need to wrap her arms around his neck and keep him in place so close to her.

Don't go, she wanted to say. But, she didn't. She held her breath as he slowly eased up into a crouch and quickly made his way to the office door.

She tensed, waiting for another gun report, praying another bullet didn't come careening out of the night toward him. She released a sigh of relief as he reached the door, unlocked it and shoved it open.

"Keep low," he said.

Keep low? She'd crawl on her belly like a worm if it kept her alive. And that's exactly what she did. As she moved, she was aware of the grit of the sidewalk beneath her, the shards of glass that littered the way.

Tension made her feel like throwing up. Somebody had shot at her. Somebody had pointed a gun and pulled the trigger. Her head pounded with the horrifying knowledge. Apparently somebody wanted her dead.

She made it to the doorway and slid inside. Joshua sat on the floor next to Raymond Buchannan's desk, the phone to his ear. As she crawled up next to him he hung up. "The sheriff is on his way. Are you okay?"

"My head hurts and my clothes are ruined, but other than being positively terrified, I think I'm fine." But, she wasn't fine. A trembling shuddered through her as she thought of the window exploding and the bullet that had caused it.

He nodded, then rising to a crouch once again he moved away from the desk and to the edge of the broken window where he peered outside. "I don't think our shooter is out there now."

"How do you know that?" Even though she wasn't at all sure she liked Joshua West that much, what she wanted to do more than anything at the moment was curl up in his arms. There was no doubt in her mind that the bullet had been meant for her.

He turned from the window and glanced back at her, his eyes glittering darkly. "If the shooter was still out there, there's no way we would have been able to make it back inside to call the sheriff. He would have fired again to try to prevent us getting help."

"What more proof do you need that something is going on? Somebody just tried to kill me and it can only be because I'm digging into things somebody doesn't want uncovered."

"Don't jump to conclusions," he replied tersely. "And when the sheriff gets here let me do the talking. If you come off like a half-hysterical female, he won't listen to either one of us."

"I've never been a hysterical female in my life," she replied with more than a touch of irritation. Now that some of the fear was passing she found herself aggravated by his words. "Part of the problem in this town is that the men don't listen to the women."

Both Meredith and Winnie had extolled Joshua's charm, but so far Savannah had seen little evidence that the man possessed any at all.

As the sound of a siren filled the night, Joshua rose to his feet, apparently convinced that whoever had shot at them was gone.

He flipped on the light and gazed around the room. Savannah remained seated on the floor. She wasn't going to stand up until Sheriff Ramsey walked into the building.

"Whoever made that shot didn't intend to kill with it," Joshua said.

She frowned. "And how do you know that?"

"Too much damage for it to have been a single bullet. It looks like it might have been birdshot, a fairly ineffective way to try to kill somebody. It can sting like hell, but usually isn't deadly, especially at this distance."

"Then maybe it was done to scare me," she said thoughtfully. "And if that was the objective, then it succeeded." She brushed off tiny pieces of glass clinging to her jeans and tried to ignore the headache that was banging at the back of her head.

The siren came closer. "This might have nothing to do with you or what you're investigating."

"Okay, then who have you pissed off since you've been back in town?" she retorted.

He didn't reply and at that moment headlights flashed through the doorway, signaling that the sheriff had arrived.

Joshua rode his horse hard, enjoying the whip of early morning wind and the sunshine that spread warmth across his back and shoulders.

Riding was one of the things he'd missed while in New York City and each morning since being back he'd started his day with a ride.

This morning, however, his mind wasn't on the joy of the massive horse beneath him or the beauty of the morning but rather on the events of the night before.

He and Ramsey had sent Savannah home, then the two men had canvassed the area, looking for clues as to where the shooter might have been standing when the trigger had been pulled.

As he'd expected, they'd found nothing. The sheriff had thought it was possible that a couple of teenage boys were responsible. He'd told Joshua that last month two of them had gotten drunk on their daddy's beer and had shot out the windows of the café in the middle of the night with a load of birdshot.

"Damn fool kids got nothing to do in this town but cause mischief," he'd said. Still, he'd promised a full investigation.

Ramsey had called Raymond Buchannan, and

when the old man had arrived they'd all worked to cover the broken window with plywood.

Ramsey might think the culprits were a couple of kids, but Savannah had been convinced that the shooting was meant to scare her off her current path. She'd reiterated before she'd left to go home that somebody better wake up and smell the coffee before more people died.

Joshua wasn't convinced that the shooter had meant to harm or scare her. He wasn't convinced the shooting was about her at all. He thought it might have been about him and that worried him.

He pulled up on the reins as he approached the stables and saw with surprise that his brother Clay was standing next to the corral gate, obviously waiting for him.

Clay opened the gate and Joshua rode through the wooden fence and directly into the stable. He dismounted, then motioned to Bobby Walker, one of the stable boys. "Bobby, you want to unsaddle and brush her down for me?"

"Sure, boss." The young man hurried over to take the reins from Joshua.

Joshua swept his hat off his head and walked out to meet his brother. "Hey bro, what are you doing here instead of having breakfast with that gorgeous fiancée of yours?"

"Just figured it was time to check in with my baby brother. I've hardly seen you since you've been back," Clay replied.

The two fell into step side-by-side as they headed for the house. "How's the wedding plans coming?" Joshua asked.

Clay winced. "For some reason I had the stupid idea that all I needed to do was hire a preacher, find a place and say I do and it would be a done deal. But women seem to have their own ideas about what should be involved when it comes to weddings."

Joshua laughed. "Libby is great, Clay. I'm happy for you." He'd met his brother's fiancée a couple of nights before, along with her daughter, Gracie. "You're going to have your hands full with that little girl. Gracie is a smart cookie and as charming as can be."

Clay smiled, his affection for the child obvious. "Yeah, she's something else. She had Smokey curled around her finger in a matter of minutes, and Dad is an absolute fool over her."

For just a moment a sharp envy shot through Joshua. He'd seen the way both eight-year-old Gracie and the beautiful Libby looked at his brother. They looked at him as if he'd hung the moon and Joshua had no doubt that the life his brother was going to share with them would be filled with plenty of love.

The last thing Joshua had been looking for in his time in New York was marriage or even a committed relationship. But since returning home and seeing his brothers with their spouses and intended spouses, he'd found himself wondering what it would be like to have a special lady in his life.

As they reached the house, Clay motioned Joshua into one of the two chairs that sat on the porch. "Let's sit and talk a bit before we go inside."

"Okay." Joshua eased down into one of the chairs as Clay sat in the other.

"It's good to have you home, Joshua. We all missed you," Clay said. "It didn't seem right whenever the family got together and you weren't there."

"Yeah, it's good to be back."

Clay stared off in the distance, a thoughtful frown wrinkling his forehead. "Actually, Dad wanted me to talk to you. He's been worried about you since you've been home."

Joshua looked at Clay in surprise. "Worried? Why?"

His brother looked at him. "He says you haven't been yourself since returning to Cotter Creek. You're quieter, more withdrawn, and he doesn't understand why you seem so adamant against working for the business."

Joshua leaned back in the chair. "I'm not totally against it, I just told him I need some time to decide exactly what I want to do."

He knew his brothers loved working for the bodyguard business and he didn't know how to explain to anyone that, for him, going back to work for that business felt like a failure.

No matter how inept, no matter how unskilled he might be, that was a job waiting for him simply by the mere accident of being born a West.

"Is there anything else going on? Anything bothering you?" Clay asked.

If Joshua was going to bare his heart to anyone in his family, it would be to Clay. The two brothers had always been close.

But the West men had never been big on soul-baring, and to be honest, Joshua was more than a little embarrassed by what had happened in New York to drive him back home. He wasn't ready to talk about it with anyone.

"I had a little excitement last night," he finally said. He explained to Clay about Savannah enlisting his aid in her quest for answers, then described the shooting that had taken place at the newspaper office.

"It was nothing but birdshot," Joshua explained.

"You think she's onto something?" Clay asked when Joshua had finished.

"I don't know," Joshua admitted thoughtfully. "It's possible what happened last night was nothing more than some kids looking for a little excitement." He released a deep sigh. "All I know for sure is that I had the feeling if I didn't agree to help her she was going to be a major pain in my ass. Have you met her?"

Clay smiled. "Yeah, Meredith introduced us to her. She seems really nice. Meredith certainly thinks the world of her."

Joshua scowled and leaned forward. "I have a feeling the woman can be stubborn as a mule, and she could definitely talk a man to death."

"Are you going to help her?"

"I told her I'd talk to Ramsey, get a copy of the reports of each incident and take a look at them for any red flags."

"You might want to talk to Zack. When Kate's father was murdered he did some investigating into some of the other deaths."

"Did he come to any conclusions?" Joshua asked.

"Apparently not."

"He told me he's thinking of running for sheriff in November."

Clay nodded. "Ramsey has said he intends to retire."

"According to Savannah he retired a long time ago and just didn't tell anyone."

Clay laughed, then sobered as he eyed his brother for a long moment. "You sure everything is all right?"

Joshua forced a grin to his lips. "You can officially report back to Dad that I'm fine. Just taking a little down time before deciding what I want to do."

Clay rose from the chair. "Don't forget you have a tuxedo fitting this afternoon. I can't have my best man looking anything but his best."

"Don't worry, I promise I won't embarrass you by turning up next weekend in anything but a well-fit tux."

Clay started for the front door. "You coming in?"

"No, I think I'll sit out here for a while."

Clay gave him a long, measured look, then went into the house, leaving Joshua alone with his thoughts.

Joshua leaned back and stared out at the pasture in the distance. He'd missed this view. It hadn't taken him long in New York City to recognize that he was a country kind of man at heart.

For a while the city had been exciting. The night-life, the fast pace, so alien from what he'd known, had invigorated him. But, after the initial novelty had worn off, he'd missed home.

He'd missed the scent of fresh hay, of green grass and cattle. But, the view wasn't all that he had missed. He'd been homesick for his brothers and his sister. Maybe because there had been no mother around, the siblings had grown up being unusually close.

But things were changing. Three of his brothers were either married or getting married. His eldest brother, Tanner, had married a princess who had come to Wild West Protective Services when renegade forces had taken over her father's kingdom.

Zach had found love with the girl next door. Kate Sampson had captured his heart while he'd helped her investigate her father's death.

And now Clay was about to take the walk down the aisle with the Hollywood beauty he'd fallen in love with. Three down, three to go, Joshua thought. He frowned as his thoughts returned to Savannah.

He needed to know if she'd uncovered something that made somebody nervous enough to take that shot the night before. The thoughts that had plagued him on his ride returned. What worried him was that it might not be about her at all.

It might be about him. He feared his problem from New York had followed him to Cotter Creek.

And if that were the case, then it was possible that just by being with her he'd put Savannah in more danger than she could ever imagine.

Chapter 5

It was just after nine when Savannah drove toward the West ranch house. She was hoping to talk Smokey into allowing her to interview him for her column. The column was due the next day and she was running out of time. Of course, she'd much prefer interviewing Joshua, but he'd made it fairly clear he wasn't interested.

Despite the horror of the night before, she'd slept like a baby. She liked to think her peaceful sleep came from the fact that whoever had shot at them had used birdshot and Joshua had told her it was obvious it wasn't meant to kill. It didn't hurt that Sheriff Ramsey had mentioned that kids had done something like that in the past.

Still, she suspected her deep sleep had been because she no longer felt so alone. At least for the moment she had Joshua on her side.

Joshua. The man was definitely under her skin, and she wasn't sure why. Granted he was nice-looking, but it was more than that. She sensed something dark in the depths of his green eyes, a torment that piqued her reporter interest.

As the West ranch came into sight she thought of the family that lived inside the house. Joshua had told her that he'd returned to Cotter Creek because he'd missed his family.

Whenever she'd spent time at the house with Meredith, she'd felt surrounded by the love the house contained, something she'd never felt in her own home.

She'd long ago come to terms with the fact that her parents had been incapable of loving her the way children needed to be loved. But that didn't mean that sometimes in the dark silent moments of the night or in a reflective pause during the day it didn't hurt.

She found it hard to imagine what the West house must have been like when there had been six small children inside. Now there was just Joshua and Meredith living at home.

Tanner and his princess bride, Anna, had built a home on the West property. Zack had moved into the Sampson home with Kate. Clay and Libby had rented a house in town until their home could be built, also on the West property, and Dalton also rented a place in town.

She had a feeling it wouldn't be long before the house would be filled with grandchildren. Already there was Gracie, Libby's little girl, and Meredith had told Savannah the other day that she suspected Anna might be pregnant.

Savannah didn't think much about marriage or having children. Certainly she would love to have both those things someday in her future, but knew better than to pine for something that might never be.

"Find a job you love, Savannah Marie," her mother had often told her. "Because your job is probably all you're going to have to fill your life."

Shoving away her mother's voice, she parked in front of the sprawling ranch house and before she got out of the car she flipped the rearview mirror into position so she could see her reflection.

She finger-combed her curls and checked her lipstick, then, realizing she was primping just in case Joshua was home, she frowned with irritation and snapped the mirror back into place.

No amount of finger-combing could transform her red curls into lush blond waves. No amount of primping could erase the freckles that danced across her nose or make the shape of her nose more elegant, her cheekbones more pronounced.

"You're plain, Savannah Marie, and you might just as well accept the idea." Her mother's voice echoed in her ears.

She grabbed her pen and notepad and got out of the car to the raucous barks of Judd and Jessie. She took a moment to pet Charlie's dogs, then went up to the porch and knocked on the door.

Red West greeted her, a broad smile lighting his features. He was a tall man, still fit despite his age although Meredith had told her he suffered from arthritis. He had all but retired from the family business, leaving it in his eldest son Tanner's hands.

"Hi, Savannah. I'm afraid you've missed Meredith. She already left to go shopping for a dress to wear to Clay's wedding."

"Actually, I'm not here to see Meredith. I'd like to talk to Smokey."

Red's eyebrows danced upward in surprise as he gestured her inside the door. "You know where to find him."

"Thanks." She walked through the large living room and into the kitchen, where Smokey sat at the kitchen table reading the morning paper.

"Too late for breakfast and too early for lunch so I can't imagine what you're doing here," he said.

She sat at the table next to him and smiled brightly, hoping she could wheedle him into the interview. "How are you doing this morning, Smokey?"

"Same as I did yesterday morning, same as I probably will be doing tomorrow morning." Smokey turned the page on the newspaper.

"I see you're enjoying this morning's issue of the *Cotter Creek Chronicle*."

"Who says I'm enjoying it?" His grizzled eyebrows drew together in a frown.

If she hadn't spent so much time at the West house she might have gotten her feelings hurt by Smokey's cantankerous attitude. But she'd been around often enough to know he talked that way to almost everyone. He seemed to take perverse pleasure in being irascible.

"Actually, I'm here on behalf of the paper," she said. "I'd like to interview you for my column on notable people in Cotter Creek."

Smokey stared at her over the edge of the paper. "Now what in God's creation makes you think I'd be interested in such nonsense."

"Give her a break, Smokey." Joshua came into the kitchen and a ridiculous wave of pleasure swept through her. He took a seat at the table opposite Savannah. "She's had a rough couple of days."

She flashed him a surprised, but grateful smile and tried to ignore the way the sight of him made her heart dance. "Come on, Smokey. I promise I'll make it as painless as possible." She tried to focus on the old man and not on Joshua, but found it impossible not to shoot surreptitious glances at the attractive cowboy.

This morning he wore a pair of jeans and a navy-blue knit shirt that clung to him in all the right places. She willed her attention back to Smokey.

He huffed a sigh and set the paper aside. "All right, but if you think you're going to make me cry like Barbara Walters always makes people cry in her interviews, you've got another thing coming."

"Great." She pulled a miniature tape recorder from her purse. "Even though I take notes, I like to make a recording as well. Is that all right with you?"

Smokey eyed the tape recorder like it was a piece of smelly trash that had somehow made its way to the table, but he nodded his head in agreement.

Savannah opened her notepad and began the interview. Initially she felt self-conscious with Joshua seated at the table, watching her with his dark green eyes.

Within minutes she forgot his presence as she talked to the cook who was not just a wounded cowboy who had no longer been able to ride the range, but a man who had stepped in for a family who was desperately in need.

She'd instinctively known the old man's story would be a good one and as he talked about the special place he'd found for himself in the West family her heart was melting for the old rascal.

It took almost an hour to get what she needed and by that time Smokey was showing definite signs of impatience to be finished.

"Thanks, Smokey. I'll just get these notes typed up and next Sunday morning everyone in town will be reading about you."

He got up from the table with a grunt. "All I care about is getting you out of my kitchen so I can get to the business of making lunch."

"You're good at that," Joshua said, falling into step with her as she left the kitchen. "You got him to talk about stuff I didn't know about him."

She smiled, a wealth of warmth sweeping through her at his compliment. "Thanks, that's my job."

"What are your plans for the rest of the day?" he asked.

"My first order of business is to get to the office and get this interview turned in," she replied. "Why?"

They stepped out on the front porch. "I was thinking maybe I'd hang out with you. You know, get an idea of a day in the life of a reporter."

She eyed him with disbelief. "You're interested in maybe becoming a reporter?"

His gaze didn't meet hers, but instead shifted out to the pastures. "No, but I'm just back in town after being gone for a while. You're relatively new to town. I just thought it might be fun to hang out together."

For just a brief second a flutter of pure feminine pleasure swept through her, but it quickly vanished beneath a dose of harsh reality.

He thought it might be fun to hang out together? This from the man who hadn't even returned her phone calls in the first three days he'd been back in town. "That's the biggest bunch of crap I've ever heard," she said flatly.

His gaze shot to her, as if her unvarnished reply had surprised him. "There's some women in this town who would probably be flattered if I told them I wanted to spend time with them."

"Yeah, well I'm not some women and I know a load of crap when I hear it. Now, are you going to tell me what's going on?"

He leaned back against the porch railing and ripped a hand through his dark hair, a frown creasing his forehead. "I've just been thinking about what happened last night and I think maybe it wouldn't hurt for me to keep an eye on you until we figure out if the shooting really was an attempt to warn you off your current path."

"So, you're offering to what? Be my personal bodyguard?"

"In an unofficial capacity," he replied.

She'd managed to minimize the danger of last night since she'd awakened this morning, but his offer of bodyguard services put a new spin on things.

"Are you sure that's necessary?" she asked.

"No, I'm not sure about much of anything. But I've always thought it was better to be safe than sorry."

"If we're talking about my safety, then I like the way you think," she said with a touch of dry humor. She wasn't sure what made her more uncomfortable, the way her heart pounded at the thought that she might be in danger, or the beat of her heart as she thought of having Joshua at her side for the next couple of days.

"Okay then." He gave a curt nod of his head as if satisfied with this new turn of events. "If you'll just wait here, I'll get my keys and things and I'll follow you back into town."

As he went back into the house, Savannah leaned against the porch railing and drew several breaths in an attempt to gain control of her racing heart.

He might not want to work for the family business, but obviously the family business was in his blood. She had to remember that he hadn't offered to spend time with her because he found her witty and charming, but rather because he thought she might be in some kind of danger.

She'd risk her life to get her story, but she certainly wasn't fool enough to risk losing her heart to a man like Joshua West.

Joshua followed behind Savannah's car in his pickup. He wasn't thrilled by his decision to act as bodyguard to her, but his personal moral code made it impossible for him not to. If he had brought danger to her, then he was responsible for keeping her safe.

It was ironic that he suspected it was possible that just by being seen with her he might have made her a target. It still stunned him, that a jilted lover could become a psychotic danger not just to him, but to a woman whose only mistake had been to be seen in his company.

He wasn't sure if he was putting Savannah into more danger by continuing to be in her company, but he was concerned that the damage had already been done. If Lauren had followed him from New York and had seen him with Savannah, then she might be in danger anyway. By playing bodyguard Joshua might make things worse, or he might just be in the right place to keep danger away from Savannah.

He patted his jacket and felt the bulk of his shoulder holster and gun beneath. He hadn't worn a gun since he'd left Cotter Creek one and a half years before. His conceal-and-carry permit was still good, and it vaguely surprised him that the weapon felt as if it belonged resting against his body.

He frowned and tightened his fingers on the steering wheel. It would be so much easier to decide on his next course of action if he knew for sure who had shot at them last night and why.

After Clay had left that morning, Joshua had gotten on his cell phone and tried to call the woman who had made his last few weeks in New York a living hell. He'd wanted to make sure she was still in New York and that she hadn't followed him here to continue her reign of torment.

Unfortunately Lauren hadn't answered the call. That didn't necessarily mean she had left New York City. She might be at work, and, although he knew she'd been a paralegal, he didn't know what law firm she worked for. He'd have to try to call again that evening.

Until he could confirm that it hadn't been her that had shot at them last night, he intended to make sure Savannah stayed safe. She shouldn't have to pay the price for his bad judgment, for his botched relationship with a nut.

He thought he'd been clear in his intentions with Lauren. He'd thought she'd understood that he was just having a good time. He'd thought she was doing the same, but she'd taken their brief relationship to heart, had manufactured it into something that had nothing to do with reality.

Then she'd gone crazy and made a scene and now he wondered just what she might be capable of. Following him here to Cotter Creek and shooting at him or at Savannah, who she might assume was his new romantic interest?

He shoved thoughts of the beautiful Lauren Edwards out of his head and tromped on the gas as he realized Savannah drove almost as fast as she talked.

When they reached the newspaper office she pulled into a parking space in front of the building and he parked next to her car.

He got out and met her on the sidewalk, where the glass from the broken window had been swept up. A new window had been installed in the storefront of the office, although it lacked the lettering that announced the place as the *Cotter Creek Chronicle*.

"While you type up your interview and do your reporter thing, I've got a couple of things to take care of here in town," he said. "I'm headed to Ramsey's office to see if I can get copies of those accident reports, then I have a fitting for my tux for Clay and Libby's wedding."

"At Henry's?" she asked. "Maybe I could go with you to your fitting? I need to get a dress."

He frowned. Although he intended to keep an eye on her and remain close, he hadn't figured on shopping with her. She must have read his hesitation on his face. "I promise I'll be quick," she hurriedly said.

"All right. I'll head over to the sheriff's office and take care of that, then I'll check back in here with you. Don't leave this building without me. Don't go to lunch, don't take a walk, don't poke your nose outside for any reason."

"Aren't you being a little drastic?"

"As I told you this morning, I'd rather err on the side of caution."

"All right, then I guess I'll see you back here in a little while."

He watched until she disappeared inside the building, then he turned and headed down the sidewalk toward the Sheriff's office. He thought she'd be safe at work with Raymond Buchannan inside with her. Lauren was crazy, but it was a devious kind of crazy. She wouldn't want witnesses around if and when she went after Savannah.

"Joshua!" A feminine voice called to him and he turned to see an obviously pregnant Melinda Kelly hurrying down the sidewalk toward him. He and Melinda had dated a couple of times before he'd gone to New York.

"I heard you were back in town." She gave him a quick hug. "You look wonderful."

"So do you," he replied with an affectionate smile. He and Melinda had shared some fun times, but there had never been that special spark between them.

"Don't lie, I look fat." She placed a hand on her burgeoning belly.

"That doesn't look like fat," he countered. "That looks like your future."

She laughed. "This baby and my husband, Jimmy, are definitely my future."

"Jimmy? You mean Jimmy McCarthy?"

She nodded. "We got married ten months ago."

"He's a good man." Jimmy McCarthy was a year younger than Joshua, and when Joshua had left town he'd been working at Mechanic's Mansion.

"He's great," she agreed, her smile reflecting a happiness Joshua had never put on her face during the time they had hung out together.

"When are you due?"

"Three more months. I've got a doctor's appointment in ten minutes, so I've got to run. It was good seeing you again, Joshua," she said, then with a warm smile she turned and went back in the direction she'd come.

Joshua watched her go, then resumed his walk in the direction of the sheriff's office. He thought of Melinda. He was glad she'd found happiness. She was a nice girl and he was pleased that she'd found a future filled with love.

And what was his future? At the moment he

didn't have a job, didn't know what he wanted to do with his life. He certainly had nobody special. He had nobody who made him happy to wake up in the morning and eager to go to bed with her at night.

Unbidden thoughts of Savannah jumped back into his head. He'd never been particularly fond of redheads, but there was something about the shade of her hair that looked warm and invited a finger to dance through the curls.

How was it possible a woman he hardly knew, a woman who talked too fast and, he suspected, had a stubborn streak a mile long had managed to get under his skin more than just a little bit? A knot formed in the pit of his stomach.

Maybe it was nothing more than he hadn't yet found his place here in town. Like Savannah, he felt like a newcomer without much of a support system other than his family.

All thoughts of Savannah fled his mind as he entered the sheriff's office. He recognized the deputy who sat at the desk in the main office. "Morning, Brody. Is Ramsey in?"

The young deputy nodded and gestured to the door in the back. "You can go on in."

Joshua gave a sharp knock on the door, then opened it to see Jim Ramsey seated at his desk, a large mug of coffee in front of him.

"I figured you'd be checking in before the morning was out," Ramsey said. "Want a cup of coffee?"

"No, thanks." Joshua sat in the chair opposite his desk. "But I do have a request for you."

"Before you make it, I should let you know that I checked in with the Rasley twins' father this morning. They were the boys that shot up the storefronts about a month ago. Anyway, they were both home all night last night. Seems they've been grounded for the last four weeks."

Joshua nodded, the knot in his stomach twisting just a little tighter. He'd hoped that the shooting last night would have an easy answer, and two ornery teenagers with a penchant for birdshot would have been the easy answer.

"What I'd like from you is a copy of all the reports for some specific accidents that have occurred in the last two years." Joshua dug the list of names that Savannah had given him out of his pocket and handed it to the portly sheriff.

Ramsey took it from him, then leaned back in his chair and frowned. "Guess Savannah Clarion has been bending your ear. She's been driving me crazy for the last couple of weeks."

Joshua offered the sheriff a conspiratorial grin. "I'd say if anyone could bend an ear, she could."

"You got that right," Ramsey returned dryly. "I got to tell you, when she first started yammering at me I pulled all those reports and looked over them again, but I didn't see anything that would make me think a conspiracy of some sort was going on."

"Would you mind me looking at them again? If I

come up with the same conclusion that you did, then maybe I can get her off both our backs."

"It will take me about an hour to pull the files and make copies. You want to wait?"

Joshua was never one to sit and cool his heels. "Nah, I'll come back for them." He stood and Ramsey did as well.

"You might tell Savannah that I haven't closed Charlie's file yet. I'm conducting a full investigation into his death, but I've got to tell you, we're a small department and there isn't much to go on."

He frowned and ran a hand through his salt and pepper hair. "I know Savannah thinks I just sit at my desk and eat doughnuts, but if I thought something bad was going on in my town, I'd be on top of it."

A few minutes later as Joshua left the office, he thought of Ramsey's words. He had no doubt that Ramsey did the best job he could as sheriff of the small town, but Cotter Creek wasn't New York City, or even Tulsa.

Most of the crime in Cotter Creek consisted of bored teenagers getting into mischief or cowboys revved up on too much beer and not enough sense.

As sheriff, Jim Ramsey hadn't had to face too many complicated or heart-stopping crimes. Joshua and his family members were far more savvy when it came to real criminals and life and death situations.

In the couple of years that Joshua had worked for the family business, he'd protected the son of a senator in Washington, D.C., against a potential kidnapping plot. He'd also spent time in Florida on a job protecting an environmentalist who had received death threats.

Joshua had liked the work, but he'd never quite gotten over the feeling that he hadn't done anything to earn his place. That was one of the reasons he'd decided to continue his education and strike out on his own.

He left the sheriff's office and decided to stop in at the Wild West Protective Services office, which was just down the street. His brother Dalton would be manning the office, and Joshua hadn't really had much of a chance to visit with him since he'd returned home.

Dalton, at thirty-three years old, was the second eldest of the siblings. Like all of them he had the dark hair and green eyes that marked him as a West. He was a quiet man, not easily riled, but with a definite stubborn streak. He'd taken over the daily running of the office duties when Tanner, Joshua's eldest brother, had gotten married almost six months before.

Dalton sat behind the desk working a crossword puzzle. "Is that what you do to get paid the big bucks?" Joshua asked.

Dalton grinned and shoved the puzzle aside. "Things have been slow the last couple of days. Seems the world is sane, at least for the moment."

"I suppose it depends on who you talk to." Joshua plopped in one of the chairs and for the next hour visited with his brother. They caught up on town gossip, discussed world politics and laughed about old times.

Afterward, Joshua returned to the sheriff's office, where Ramsey had the paperwork ready for him. By that time it was almost noon. Joshua returned to the newspaper office to check in on Savannah.

"I'm so glad you're here," she exclaimed the moment he walked through the door. "I'm starving. How about we get some lunch, then head over to Henry's?"

The tension that always seemed to fill him when she was around kicked in once again. "Okay. Sunny Side Up Café?"

"As if there's any other choice in this town for lunch," she replied with one of those quicksilver grins that warmed her features.

As they walked down the sidewalk toward the café, Joshua kept an eye on their surroundings, noting the people on the streets, looking for a particular person who didn't belong.

It disturbed him that despite the scent of fall that rode the air he could smell Savannah's perfume, that intoxicating fragrance that seemed to permeate his entire head.

"I finished up the column on Smokey. I think it came out great," she said as they walked. "Thanks for helping me convince him to be interviewed."

He cast her a rueful smile. "I have a feeling he was secretly pleased. If he hadn't really wanted to be interviewed, then nothing you or I could say would have made him agree."

"Was Sheriff Ramsey cooperative when you spoke to him about getting those reports?"

He nodded. "I have them in my truck. I'll go over them this evening and let you know what I find."

"Why can't we go over them together this afternoon? I'm finished with my work for the day." She bobbed her head, red curls dancing. "Yes, I really think we should go over them together."

They entered the Sunny Side Up Café, and Joshua led her toward a booth in the back where he slid into the side facing the front door of the restaurant and she sat across from him.

It was almost noon and the place was quickly filling with the lunch crowd. He cast a quick, assessing glance around the room, noting that most all of the faces of the diners were familiar ones.

If it wasn't for the woman seated across from him he'd relax, but he was aware of her gaze on him as he reached for one of the two menus propped up on the side of the table.

"This place always smells yummy, doesn't it?" she said once they were settled. "Scottsdale has a hundred fine restaurants, but none of them smell as good as this café."

"I missed the food here almost as much as I missed Smokey's cooking," he replied.

"Don't you want to take your jacket off?" she asked. "It's pretty warm in here."

"I need to keep it on." He moved one side of the jacket aside so she could see the shoulder holster and gun beneath.

Her pretty eyes widened. "Is that really necessary?"

"I don't intend to get shot at again without having the potential to return fire if needed." He let the jacket fall back into place and stared down at the menu.

His thoughts filled with the woman he'd left behind in New York, a woman who had developed a fatal attraction for him. He'd seen what she was capable of, knew the bitter hatred that now burned in her heart for him.

If she'd followed him here to Cotter Creek and if she had gotten it into her head that Savannah meant anything to him, then Savannah was at risk. He touched his jacket and felt the reassuring bulk of the gun.

Was the gun necessary? What he feared was that it might be the only thing that stood between Savannah and danger, and he hoped if it came to that he'd be able to use the gun on a woman he'd slept with in order to save a woman he wasn't even sure he liked.

Chapter 6

It was during lunch that Savannah saw flashes of the charm Winnie and Meredith had told her Joshua possessed.

They swapped stories, her telling him a little about her life in Scottsdale and him telling her about New York City.

The conversation was light and easy, but something about him intrigued Savannah like no man had intrigued her in a very long time.

When they'd finished lunch they went directly to Henry's, where Joshua disappeared into a back room to be fitted for his tux and she surfed the racks looking for a perfect dress to wear to the wedding.

She found a buttercup-yellow dress with classic

lines and bought it off the rack. She'd done enough shopping to know what style looked best on her and what size to buy. By that time Joshua was finished with his fitting.

"Why don't we go to my place to go over the reports?" she said as they left Henry's.

"What's wrong with the newspaper office?"

"Mr. Buchannan doesn't exactly support my investigative efforts. I've got a little office at Winnie's. We can work there." His face radiated reluctance. "What's the matter Joshua, afraid I'll jump your bones if we're alone?"

He looked at her in surprise. "Why would I think that?"

"I'm sure a guy who looks like you is accustomed to women wanting to jump your bones, but I promise you I'll restrain any impulses in that direction."

He obviously recognized that she was teasing him, trying to keep things light between them. "And what makes you think I'd want you to restrain yourself?" he countered with a slow, sexy grin.

A rush of heat swept through her and she decided she liked him better when he was taciturn. That smile of his could definitely be dangerous for it made her think all kinds of inappropriate thoughts.

"Give me a break," she retorted, sorry she'd started the stupid conversation in the first place. "Shall we ride together to Winnie's or do you just want to follow me?"

"I'll follow you."

Minutes later as she drove toward Winnie's house, her thoughts filled with Joshua West. She couldn't seem to get a handle on him.

He'd been a pleasant lunch companion and yet there was a darkness that clung to him, a darkness that pulled her closer with a desire to understand.

She had the feeling he'd agreed to investigate the deaths of the area more in an effort to get her off his back than because he believed anything suspicious was going on in the town.

He'd definitely surprised her with his offer to act as personal bodyguard until they knew what was going on.

It gave her investigation more substance, as had the shooting the night before. She was eager to go over those reports.

She'd requested them from Sheriff Ramsey a little over a week ago but he'd put her off, telling her he didn't have the manpower for somebody to stand around and make copies all day long. Funny that he'd managed to get it done for a West.

But the thought of going through those reports wasn't what prompted the tingle that danced across her skin or the wave of heat that warmed her insides like a jigger of whiskey swallowed in one gulp. Those particular physical sensations came strictly from the thought of spending more time with Joshua.

For just a moment she'd flirted with him with her comment about restraining herself from jumping his bones. But he'd flirted back, and from that point on she'd had difficulty concentrating on anything except the memory of that sexy grin that had curved his lips.

By nature she'd never been a flirt, but something about Joshua made her wish she were adept at a little harmless feminine flirtation. She could get used to that smile of his.

She pulled into Winnie's driveway and parked, aware of Joshua's pickup pulling in behind her. *Stay focused on the business,* she commanded herself.

His darkly lashed green eyes or his handsome chiseled features couldn't distract her. She couldn't allow herself to dwell on the sexy curve of his mouth or that lingering vision of him shirtless. She knew to indulge in any of these kinds of thoughts where Joshua West was concerned was to invite in certain heartache. And she was a champion at guarding her heart.

Together they went into the attractive two-story house where Winnie had lived with her late husband for forty years. Winnie greeted them in the living room, where she was seated in her favorite chair with her quilting frame in front of her.

She stood and smiled at Joshua, obviously delighted to see him. "Joshua West," she exclaimed and walked over to give him a hug.

"If it isn't the most beautiful lady in Cotter Creek," he said as he released her.

Winnie slapped his chest playfully and giggled with uncharacteristic girlish delight. "Of all you West boys, you were always the one most full of charmer beans. I'm glad to see New York City didn't change that."

"I've got to admit, it's good to be home," he said.

"I'll bet your family is glad to have you back. I know your daddy worried about you all the time while you were gone."

A slight frown creased his brow. "He had nothing to worry about. I'm capable of taking care of myself."

"Well, of course you are," Winnie agreed.

"We've got some work to do," Savannah explained to Winnie. "I thought we could work in the office upstairs, if that's all right with you."

"That upstairs is your home, honey. You don't have to get my permission to have a man up there," Winnie said. "In fact, I'd say it's high time. It's not right, a nice girl like you not having any male callers."

A warmth of embarrassment swept into Savannah's cheeks. Without glancing toward Joshua, she started for the staircase. "Let's get to work," she said briskly.

The upstairs of Winnie's house consisted of three bedrooms and a bath. When Savannah had moved in one of the bedrooms had been empty and it was that room she had set up as a home office.

The desk was actually an old square table that Winnie had stored in her basement. Savannah's laptop sat on top, along with a silver frame containing a photo of her parents and a crystal bowl holding a couple of candy bars.

"It's not much, but at least we'll have room to spread out those reports," she said and motioned him to one of the two straight-back chairs that were at the table. She moved her laptop and the other items off the table and to the floor next to her.

He eased down into one of the chairs and gazed at her with a raised dark eyebrow. "Cotter Creek is full of lonely cowboys. You've been in town several months and I'm the first man you've had here? Why is that?"

She sat across from him and returned his gaze. "Let's face it, Joshua. I'm not the prettiest crayon in the box. My mother told me it was important that I compensate for that fact by being well-groomed, sweet-natured and a good listener. I got the good grooming part down, but I'm not particularly sweet-natured. I talk too much, I'm abrasive, aggressive and I think I scare the hell out of most of the lonely cowboys in this town."

Amusement lit his eyes and he grinned that lazy smile. "You don't scare me a bit."

Oh, but he scared her. He scared her with his bedroom eyes and the deep languid tone of his voice when he was teasing. He scared her because he made her wish she were something other than what she was.

"Let's get to work," she exclaimed, irritated with him but even more irritated with herself.

For the next three hours they pored over the

reports, looking for anything that might support her theory that the deaths ruled as accidents weren't what they appeared to be.

Tension made her shoulders ache and a faint headache pounded just behind her eyes. She knew that Joshua's assessment would determine whether she was written off as a nut or taken seriously.

He said little as he read each of the reports carefully, occasionally reaching for a pen and underlining a sentence. She had to bite her bottom lip to keep from asking him what he was underlining, what was he thinking? She had a feeling the more questions she asked, the less likely he would be to see things her way.

Already she sensed he was not a man who was easily pushed, and she knew if he made up his mind that she was wasting his time, then she'd get no other opportunity to sway him differently.

The scents of dinner wafted up the stairs when Joshua finally set the last report aside and leaned back in his chair with a sigh.

"I don't know," he said slowly. "You're right, there are some small red flags, but nothing that absolutely jumps out and screams foul."

A wave of disappointment swept over her. "So, you think I'm just a nut." She reached down beside her chair and grabbed one of her candy bars. She offered it to him, but when he declined she ripped the paper off with a vengeance and took a bite.

He grinned. "Yeah, I think you're probably a nut,

but I also think there's enough questions that I'd like to dig into these accidents a little further."

She flashed him a smile of relief, hoping she didn't have gooey chocolate decorating her teeth. "For real?"

"Don't get too excited," he warned her as he stood. "I'm still not convinced that there's anything here." He glanced at his watch, then back at her. "What are your plans for the rest of the evening?"

"Probably the same as they are for most nights. Winnie and I will probably play a couple of games of rummy, then I'll work a little bit on a couple of stories for the paper."

"Until we have a handle on why we got shot at, I'd prefer you not go out anywhere alone."

"Okay," she agreed. Although she didn't like curtailing her freedom, she also didn't intend to be stupid enough not to heed his warning.

Together they walked down the stairs. Winnie had apparently abandoned her sewing for dinner preparations and the scents emanating from the kitchen were heavenly.

"You want to stay for dinner?" she asked. "Winnie always makes plenty."

He shook his head. "Thanks, but I need to get back to the ranch. What time are you planning on going into the office tomorrow?" he asked as they stepped out on the front porch.

"Actually, I hadn't planned on going in until the afternoon. Mrs. Miller is having a breakfast for her garden party in the morning and I'm supposed to attend and write up the affair. Garden parties, funerals, weddings, whenever there's a social affair, I'm the reporter on record."

"And you're satisfied with that?" he asked.

"Of course not," she replied honestly. "But, it's enough for now. My real goal is to get Buchannan to sell me the paper when he decides to retire."

He smiled. "You think he'll really sell?"

She shrugged, acutely aware of his nearness on the small porch. "He says he might be interested in retiring by next spring and we might be able to work out a deal."

"Then you intend to still be in town next spring?" He moved a step closer to her, so close she could smell his scent, feel the heat of his body.

"Don't listen to the rumors you hear about me trying to make some kind of a name for myself here then going to a bigger city, a bigger newspaper. I could have stayed in Scottsdale and gotten a job there, but that wasn't what I wanted." She was rambling again, nervous by his nearness, disturbed by it.

"And what do you want?" he asked in a low voice.

You. The word jumped into her mind. Just for a minute. No, just for a night. A long night of crazy lovemaking, of total abandonment. God, what was wrong with her?

"I guess I want what everyone wants," she said quickly. "Happiness and a sense of purpose. Good health and friends I can count on." She sounded lame. "What about you? What do you want, Joshua?"

"At the moment I can just think of one thing I want." He stared at her mouth for a long moment, then leaned in and captured it with his.

He didn't know why in the hell he'd decided to kiss her, other than the fact that she had looked so damned kissable. Her lips were soft and yielding and her mouth tasted of just a hint of chocolate.

She leaned into him, her full breasts pressing against his chest and the contact shot a fierce wave of heat through him. What he wanted was to wrap his arms around her and pull her tight against him. What he wanted was to take her clothes off and see if the rest of her tasted as sweet as her mouth.

He broke the kiss and stepped back from her, irritated by his own actions.

"I didn't mean to do that." He glared at her, finding her personally responsible for his own lapse in judgement.

She returned his gaze coolly. "Don't worry, it will be our little secret. I won't tell anyone you kissed the plain conspiracy theorist who has been driving everyone crazy with questions." She released a sigh. "So what happens now, and I'm not talking about after a kiss. What happens in our investigation? What's our next step?"

He wanted to say something to take the sting out

of her words. He wanted to tell her she wasn't plain at all, but he had a feeling saying anything like that would only complicate the whole situation. "We'll talk about it tomorrow. What time is your breakfast thing?" All he wanted was to get away from her with her sexy smell and kissable lips.

"Nine."

"Then I'll pick you up around eight-thirty." With these final words he turned and left the porch.

Minutes later as he headed back to the family ranch, he wondered again why he'd kissed her. Maybe it was because he'd spent the last several hours cooped up in a small room with her.

He'd been intensely aware of her physical presence, the scent of her, the soft sighs that occasionally escaped her while reading those reports. More than once he'd watched her run a finger across her lower lip when she was concentrating, a gesture he found both enticing and irritating.

He had no idea how she could really consider herself plain. Plain was boring and there was nothing remotely boring about the way that Savannah Clarion looked.

Okay, so he'd made a mistake and kissed her. No harm. No foul. He just needed to make sure he didn't do it again. The last thing he wanted to do was repeat the mistakes of his past. He didn't want her to mistake a single, stupid kiss for something more.

He shoved thoughts of the kiss aside and instead thought about the reports he'd read throughout the afternoon. He didn't know if Savannah was really onto something or if somehow she'd managed to suck him into her delusion.

He remembered Clay mentioning that Zack and Kate had done some investigating when Kate's father had been murdered and decided to swing by the Sampson ranch on his way home.

As he pulled up in front of the ranch house he saw his brother and Kate seated on the front porch swing. Zack stood up as Joshua got out of his truck.

"Well, well, look what the wind blew in," he said.

"Hi, Zack, Kate." He smiled at his pretty sister-in-law. "You two got a few minutes?"

"Sure, come on in," Kate said. "I was just about to fix us some coffee."

Together the three of them went inside and to the kitchen, where Zack and Joshua sat at the table and Kate made the coffee.

"So, when are you coming back to work for the agency?" Zack asked the minute they got settled in the chairs.

Joshua frowned, tamping down an edge of irritation. "Why does everyone keep asking me that? Why does everyone just assume that's what I'm going to do?"

Zack leaned back in his chair and eyed his brother in surprise. "I never understood why you wanted to do anything else. You might have been a good stock-broker, but you were a terrific bodyguard."

Joshua waved his hand as if to physically dismiss the compliment. That's what family did, told you that you were good no matter what the truth was. "Actually, what I wanted to talk to you about was the investigation you did when Gray was killed."

Kate carried coffee to the table and set a cup in front of each of the men, then slid into a chair next to Zack. "What do you want to know?" she asked.

She was a pretty woman, with long reddish-brown hair. The red shades of her hair reminded him of Savannah and that damned kiss they had shared. He shoved the memory of that brief but hot kiss aside to focus on the questions he wanted to ask.

Briefly he told them about Savannah's suspicions and the shooting at the newspaper office. When he was finished, a deep frown cut across Zack's forehead.

"After Gray's death we found out that not only had Sonny Williams killed Gray, but he'd also tried several times to kill Katie." He reached over and took his wife's hand in his as if to assure himself that she was fine.

She flashed Zack a quick smile, then looked at Joshua. "We also found out that a deposit of a hundred thousand dollars had been deposited in Sonny's bank account on the day my dad was killed."

Joshua released a small whistle. "That's not exactly chicken feed."

Zack nodded. "We tried to chase down the source of the money, but we hit dead ends everywhere we turned."

"When Sonny was arrested and before he was led away to jail he told us that my father's death wasn't anything personal, that it was strictly business," Kate said. "We've tried to follow up on what he meant, what it all means, but like Zack said, we've hit nothing but dead ends."

Joshua wrapped his hands around the coffee mug. "But what you've told me definitely lends credence to Savannah's notion that something is going on in this town."

Zack and Kate exchanged glances and Zack nodded. "We've felt the same way, but we haven't been able to get to the bottom of things."

"Besides, we've been pretty busy here at the ranch," Kate added. "When Dad died the ranch was in a bad financial state. Things had been neglected and it's taken all of our time and energy to get things back into shape." Once again she reached for Zack's hand. "We're slowly getting things back to what they once were, but it's been a struggle."

"After Gray's death and Sonny's arrest I talked to Jim Ramsey about my concerns and left it at that," Zack explained.

Joshua sipped his coffee, his thoughts racing in half a dozen directions. Was Savannah right? Was she really onto something? A plot that had somebody killing the ranchers in Cotter Creek and making the deaths look like accidents? It sounded plumb crazy.

Had somebody killed Charlie and made it look like the old man had eaten his gun? But why? Why would anyone do such things?

"So, you never figured out why Sonny killed Gray?" he asked.

Kate shook her head. "That's been one of the most difficult things of all, not knowing why Dad was killed or why Sonny tried to kill me."

"Maybe it's time somebody gets to the bottom of all this," Joshua said thoughtfully.

"Let us know if there's anything we can do to help." A hardness swept into Zack's green eyes. "There's nothing we'd like more than to find out who was really responsible for Gray's death. We know Sonny did the actual murder, but somebody paid him a lot of money to do the deed. That's the person I want."

Joshua nodded, finished his coffee, then stood. "I'd better get out of here and let you two enjoy the rest of your evening."

"I'll walk you out." Zack rose as well and the two men walked back outside.

Of all the brothers, Zack and Joshua were the most alike in temperament. Zack was impulsive, quick to anger but equally quick to forgive. He was passionate about things he cared about, passionate about his convictions.

Zack walked with him to the pickup. "There's been a lot of speculation that you're going to run for sheriff in the fall," Joshua said.

"It's not speculation, it's fact. Ramsey intends to retire and I'd like to take over his job."

"So, you'll quit working for Wild West Protective Services?"

Zack hesitated a moment, then nodded. "I feel like I've got more to offer to this town as sheriff than I'm willing to offer to the business." He glanced back toward the house. "I loved working as a bodyguard, but I'm not willing to travel anymore. My life now is here with Katie."

There was a quiet happiness in Zack's voice that shot an unexpected wave of envy through Joshua. "I think you'll make a great sheriff."

Zack grinned. "Thanks, brother. I appreciate the vote of confidence."

As Joshua drove home he thought about that unexpected emotion. What was it about seeing his brothers' happiness with their wives that made him wish he had something like that in his own life?

Why now? When his life was so unsettled, when he had no real direction, when he was confused by who he was, separate and apart from being a West?

As he pulled up in front of the West ranch house he consciously willed his disturbing thoughts about relationships and his brothers away.

He wasn't ready for a relationship with any woman. If he had learned nothing else in New York, he'd learned that he didn't know how to handle women.

All he had to figure out was how to get through this investigation with Savannah, keep her safe from harm and not do anything stupid that would only complicate his life.

Chapter 7

Savannah stood in front of her bathroom mirror and stared at her reflection. The yellow dress she'd bought for Clay and Libby's wedding had been a good choice. It fit her figure as if it had been specifically made for her and the color complemented both her skin tone and her red curls.

Joshua should be here within the next fifteen minutes or so to pick her up and take her to the wedding. This afternoon Clay would marry the woman he loved and another of the West men would be permanently off the dating market.

Joshua. She turned away from the mirror and returned to the bedroom where she sat on the edge of her bed.

Joshua. The past week spent in his company had been both the most exhilarating and the most frustrating she'd ever spent in her life.

Exhilarating because something about him made her heart beat just a little bit faster, made her breath come with a little more difficulty. His slow, sexy smiles didn't come frequently, but when he gifted her with one, it sizzled through her.

She'd learned many things about Joshua West. He didn't like to talk about himself. He had a self-confidence that at times bordered arrogance, and sometimes when he looked at her he made her forget that she wasn't beautiful.

They'd argued politics, talked about movies and shared a fondness for apple pie and ice cream. She knew him better after the short time than she'd ever known another man in her life, and yet there were parts of him that were definitely a mystery.

She'd asked him several times to let her interview him for her column. She believed everyone would find him an interesting profile as many of the people of Cotter Creek would never get close to living in a big city like New York. But he continued to refuse.

They had spent the week digging further into the accidental deaths that had plagued the area for the past two years, but they had come up with nothing to sink their teeth in.

She felt as if somehow they were missing something, overlooking a fact that would make everything make sense. But for the life of her she couldn't figure out what that might be.

She was frustrated with their failure to make any progress on the investigation but her real frustration came from the fact that each moment they were together she felt a tension that neared explosive proportions.

She wanted him. Whenever she was with him her desire for him made it difficult for her to think of anything else. She wanted him and she knew nothing good could come from it.

It had been over a week and nothing more had happened to make her think she might be in any danger. She'd definitely begun to believe that the shooting that night at the newspaper office was either the work of a drunk or bored kids looking for a little excitement.

After the wedding this afternoon she intended to tell Joshua that his bodyguard responsibilities weren't needed any longer. It was getting more and more difficult to spend time around him and not think about that kiss.

That kiss. That brief, unexpected kiss that had rocked her world, weakened her knees and made her want more from him than he would ever be willing to give to her.

Yes, it was time she gained some distance from him and she intended to tell him. Glancing at her dainty gold wristwatch she realized it was time for him to arrive.

"Don't you look beautiful," Winnie exclaimed as Savannah came down the stairs.

"Thanks. You look very nice, too." Winnie was clad in a light blue dress with lacy accents. She was riding to the wedding with her best friend, Lillian Walker, who worked as the Cotter Creek city clerk. "I think everyone in town has been invited," she said as she grabbed a matching beaded blue purse from the coffee table.

"Are you all going to the reception afterward?" Savannah asked. The wedding was taking place at two, and at four there was to be a huge reception at the West ranch.

"I wouldn't miss it," Winnie said. "Red and Smokey know how to throw a party." A honk from the driveway interrupted their conversation. Winnie looked out the window. "That's Lillian."

"Go on, I'll lock up," Savannah assured her. "We'll see you at the church."

She watched as Winnie joined Lillian in the car and they pulled out of the driveway and disappeared down the street. At the same time Joshua's pickup appeared and pulled into the driveway.

She didn't wait for him to get out of the truck, but instead grabbed her purse, locked the door and ran out to meet him.

The minute she saw him in the black tux with the cranberry-colored cummerbund and matching bow tie, the same crazy tension that had been present all week long renewed itself.

She'd seen him in jeans and knit shirts, she'd seen him in dress slacks and sports jackets, but nothing had prepared her for Joshua West in a tux.

"You look gorgeous," she blurted out as he backed out of the driveway.

"Thanks, you look pretty hot yourself," he returned with an easy grin.

Of course, she knew it was a lie, but she appreciated the effort on his part. "It's a gorgeous day for a wedding," she said. "Of course, as far as I'm concerned there isn't a bad day for a wedding."

"Is that what you're waiting for? A wedding day?"

"Sure, someday I'd like to get married and have a family, but I'm not looking to make it happen anytime soon. I'm young and I'm not in a hurry. In fact, that's the last thing on my mind these days. What about you?"

"Definitely not in the market for either." He said the words fiercely, as if to let her know exactly where he stood on the matter. "There are some guys meant for happily ever after. I'm not one of them, at least not at this point in my life."

"Don't worry, Joshua. You aren't my type anyway," she said lightly. "When I decide to get married, I'd like the bride to be prettier than the groom and in our case that just doesn't work."

He cast her a sideways glance. "Why do you do that?"

"Do what?"

"Why do you put yourself down like that?"

She flushed slightly. "I'm not putting myself down, I just don't suffer any illusions about myself. I know who I am and what I have to offer. I know my strengths and my weaknesses." She definitely knew her weaknesses, having them cataloged by her mother from the time she was a child.

He pulled into the church parking lot. He said nothing until he'd parked the truck and turned off the engine, then he turned and looked at her, his gaze enigmatic. "You want to know what I think? I think somebody definitely did a number on you and you don't have a clue what your strengths are."

He didn't wait for her reply, but got out of the truck and slammed the door with more force than necessary. Moody. Definitely, the man was moody.

As they walked toward the front of the church Savannah found herself wondering about the darkness she sensed in Joshua.

There were times when his eyes were shadowed with emotion she didn't understand, and it surprised her that she wanted to know the root of that darkness. It surprised her that she was as attracted to the inner man as she was to his outward appearance.

She found a seat in one of the back pews as Joshua disappeared to find the rest of the wedding party. She'd meet up with him again after the ceremony and they'd go together back to the West ranch for the reception.

As she waited for things to begin, she pulled out

a small notepad and made notes that would become an article for the paper.

White and burgundy roses bedecked the church, their beauty so intense it created a small ache inside her. Scented candles were lit, their flickering glows completing the romantic ambience.

When the men took their places near the minister and the traditional music began to play, a swell of emotion filled her.

Weddings always made her cry and the tears began the minute Libby's daughter, Gracie, began her walk down the aisle as flower girl. She looked like a miniature fairy princess in a billowing white dress and with her pale blond hair falling in ringlets down her back. As she walked and dropped rose petals, she smiled at the man who would be her official daddy when the ceremony was finished.

Clay stood at the front of the church, his brothers beside him as groomsmen. Her gaze lingered on Joshua, who looked slightly ill at ease but handsome as the devil. Clay smiled at the little flower girl, and she hurried her footsteps, almost skipping toward him.

As the bridesmaids began their march down the aisle her throat closed up as her tears increased. Meredith was first, looking more lovely and put together than Savannah had ever seen her. Then came Kate and Anna and another woman Savannah didn't recognize. One more lovely than the next in their cranberry-colored dresses and with flowers decorating their hair.

By the time Libby appeared in a stunning wedding gown and made her regal walk toward Clay, Savannah dug into her purse for a tissue.

Clay's face lit at the sight of his bride, his gaze filled with such love it was palpable in the air.

It was at that moment Savannah knew she'd lied to Joshua. She'd basically told him that love and marriage wasn't important to her, but that wasn't true.

There was a deep core of loneliness inside her, one that had ached inside her for as long as she could remember. She wanted somebody in her life, somebody who would listen to her dreams and share her desire.

She was filled with the need to love, with the desire to be loved. And her greatest fear was that she'd never find her lonely cowboy, she'd never get the opportunity to see a man look at her as Clay looked at Libby.

Her greatest fear was that her mother had been right when she'd told Savannah that she'd better learn to be content alone because a happily-ever-after probably wasn't in her future.

The white canopy shielded the wedding guests from the late afternoon sun. Beneath the canopy were tables and chairs and enough food to feed two townships.

Joshua stood near one of the food tables, a soft drink in his hand, his bow tie dangling loose. It appeared that the whole town was here. Mayor Aaron Sharp was holding court at one of the tables, talking to several other members of the city council. Jim Ramsey sat with a couple of his deputies, looking relaxed and definitely off duty.

Red and Smokey bustled between the kitchen and the tables, making sure the platters of food remained heaping and everyone got their fill.

A local band provided the music and a wooden dance floor had been laid out on the grass. A dozen couples occupied the space, two-stepping to a Garth Brooks tune. One of those couples was his brother Dalton and Savannah.

She looked like a bright yellow daisy, warm and vibrant amid the other people on the dance floor. Yellow was definitely a good color on her.

He narrowed his gaze as he watched them dance. It was obvious Savannah didn't know how to two-step and each time she messed up she raised her head to look at Dalton and laughed.

Heat coiled in Joshua's stomach, a familiar heat that he felt each time he looked at her. If only he hadn't kissed her. The kiss had been a momentary lapse of judgment he'd paid for ever since with a heightened sense of sexual desire for her.

Over the last week he'd learned several things about Savannah Clarion. She was smart and confident when she was working. She was good with people and had a sense of humor most people would envy.

But, even though she had a bravado about her, he sensed her insecurity as a woman. She obviously had no idea that she possessed an earthy sexiness that was far more interesting than traditional beauty.

She seemed to have no idea that when she smiled she lit from within and that whoever was gifted with that smile felt special. More than once she'd repeated something her mother had said to her and Joshua wouldn't have minded taking her mother out and horse-whipping her for the insecurities she'd put in Savannah's head.

Damn the woman anyway. He turned his back on the dance floor and instead eyed the faces of the crowd, seeking one who didn't belong, one who might have hatred in her heart.

For the past week he'd tried to connect with Lauren, to assure himself that she was still in New York City and not someplace in Cotter Creek.

Unfortunately, he'd been unable to get in touch with her. Her answering machine picked up at her house no matter what time he'd tried to call. She was either not home or not taking calls.

He'd also made several calls to mutual friends they had shared, but none of those friends had been able to tell him where she was or what she might be doing. Nobody had seen her at the usual places for the past week.

It had been a frustrating week on all levels as far as Joshua was concerned. He'd not only fought against his own desire for Savannah and failed at finding out what Lauren might be up to, but their investigation had stalled as well.

They had spent the week getting in touch with family members of the victims of the accidental deaths. Most had moved away, others weren't interested in rehashing the tragedies and nothing they had learned had indicated there was foul play at hand.

And yet despite that they'd hit nothing but dead ends, over the past week Joshua's instincts had begun to whisper that maybe Savannah was right. Maybe something bad was happening in the town he loved.

It was Charlie's death that made him believe something wasn't right. As the week had progressed and he'd gained some emotional distance from the trauma of finding Charlie dead, he'd found it hard to believe that Charlie would have done such a thing under his own volition.

Although his logic battled with his instinct, he'd decided to go with his instinct for the moment. He glanced back at Savannah, who had changed partners and was now dancing with Joe Steward, a middle-aged widower with four kids at home.

Joshua thought about cutting in, but the idea of holding Savannah in his arms, feeling her lush curves against him sent an uncomfortable shot of desire through him.

"Heard you're moving."

Joshua turned and smiled at his brother Zack. "Yeah, I've decided to move into the cabin." The cabin was a little two-bedroom place down the lane from the big house. At one time or another almost all the brothers had lived there. Zack had been the last and had left to move in with Kate.

"Any reason why you decided to make the move?"

"Nothing in particular. I just got used to having my own space while I was in New York." Certainly that was part of the reason he'd decided to move, but not the main one.

Each time his father looked at him Joshua felt a silent pressure to bend to his father's will, to agree to go back into the family business.

"You need help moving your things?" Zack asked.

"Nah, it's just a matter of taking a couple of suit-cases to the cabin." At that moment Kate joined them.

"Hey, Joshua, you look as handsome as ever," she said. "All you Wests look fine in a tux."

Zack tugged at his collar. "Personally, I can't wait to get out of this monkey suit."

"I couldn't agree more," Joshua said with a laugh.

"If you'll excuse us, I believe my husband has promised me at least one spin around the dance floor." Kate grabbed Zack's hand, who moaned loudly but allowed his wife to pull him to the dance floor.

Once again his attention was captured by Savannah, who was twirling on the arm of yet another man. Didn't the woman ever take a break? She'd been dancing nonstop almost since the moment the band had begun playing.

"Nice party."

Joshua turned to see a familiar face. "Hi, Ms. Burnwell," he said to the flashy-dressed woman who worked as a Realtor in Cotter Creek.

"It's Wadsworth now, Sheila Wadsworth." She smiled. "While you were in New York I went and got myself married."

"Congratulations," Joshua replied. "Have you retired from the real estate business?"

"Heavens, no, I'm busier than I've ever been. Thomas, that's my husband, he's always complaining that the only way he can get any attention from me is if he wears a For Sale sign around his neck. And speaking of Thomas, I'd better go find him. That man has an unusual fondness for the spiked punch."

As she hurried off Joshua stared after her. So, the real estate business was booming in Cotter Creek. He frowned, a thought niggling at the back of his head. As the thought took full form, he looked around for Savannah.

He spied her on the dance floor with yet another partner, a young man he didn't recognize. Her cheeks were flushed with color and she looked at Joshua in surprise as he tapped her partner on the shoulder. "I'm taking your partner," he said to the young man.

He frowned, but stepped back. Joshua grabbed Savannah's hand and led her off the dance floor. "What are you doing?" she asked.

"I've thought of something and we need to check it out." He pulled her away from the party and toward his truck.

"What? What did you think of? Where are we going?" She hurried to keep up with his long strides.

"We need to find a plat of the area. I have a hunch."

"I have a plat in my office at Winnie's."

He got into the truck and started the engine as she scrambled into the seat next to him. "What's your hunch?" she asked as they pulled away from the West ranch.

"I'll tell you when we get that plat." He might be wrong. He needed to visually see on paper what was in his mind at the moment. "You looked like you were having fun." He cast a quick glance at her, noting that her cheeks still held a flush of color and her eyes sparkled brightly.

"I love to dance. I'm not terrific at it, but I love it. The wedding was wonderful, wasn't it? Libby looked like a fairy princess."

As they drove to Winnie's place she continued to chatter about the wedding, talking about how cute Gracie had looked, the decorations in the church and how happy the bride and groom had appeared.

He thought he heard a wistful note in her voice but told himself all women got a little silly when it came to weddings and babies.

By the time they reached Winnie's, he was as tense as he'd ever been. He told himself it had nothing to do with Savannah, that he was anxious to see if his suppositions were right. If what he believed was correct, then Savannah wasn't crazy and there was something wicked going on in Cotter Creek.

Savannah unlocked the front door, then led him up the staircase. He followed behind her, trying not to notice the sway of her shapely bottom mere inches in front of his face as they climbed the stairs.

Once they were in the room she used as an office, he stood in the doorway and watched as she dug through a pile of papers stacked in one corner.

"I know I've got one somewhere," she said as she flipped through the stack. "I got one from Lillian down at City Hall when I first arrived in town. It made it easier for me to know where everyone lived when I needed to conduct interviews. Ah, here it is."

She straightened and unfolded the large plat and laid it on the table. Joshua walked over and looked at the map that detailed the lots and land of Cotter Creek and the immediate surrounding area.

As he focused on the map, he tried not to notice the disturbing scent of her, a fragrance that smelled clean and fresh with just a hint of vanilla and musk. He grabbed a pen, then looked at her. "Who was the first person who died in a suspicious accident?"

"George Townsend. A kerosene heater exploded and his place burned down, him with it."

Joshua looked at the plat and placed a big *X* on the Townsend property. "Who's next?"

"Roy Nesmith. He fell out of his hayloft."

Joshua identified the Nesmith property and placed a large *X* there. One by one they went through the names and marked the property, with Charlie's land being the last on their list.

"Oh, my God," Savannah said softly as they both stared at the plat. The marked areas formed a disturbing pattern. All the accidental deaths took place on the west side of town.

"What do you think the odds of something like this happening are?" he asked. "That all the accidents would happen to men who lived in the same area?"

Savannah's eyes were wide as she held his gaze. "It's about the land, isn't it?" She looked down at the plat, then back at him, her breasts rising and falling with quickened breaths.

"It has to be about the land." Without warning she threw her arms around his neck. "You did it! I knew you could help me figure it out."

The moment her arms curled around his neck, the instant her breasts made contact with his chest, he lost the ability to figure out anything. All he knew was that she was warm in his arms and that since the last time he'd kissed her all he'd thought about was when he might kiss her again.

She must have seen something in his eyes, something that should have made her dance away from him, but instead she pressed closer into him and parted her lips as if in invitation.

He couldn't help but respond. He'd been on the verge of an explosion for the past week. As he crashed his mouth down to hers, he allowed the explosion to consume him.

Chapter 8

Savannah felt as if she'd waited a lifetime for his kiss. There was a hot, hungry demand in his lips that forced all thoughts of crazy conspiracies and land schemes out of her mind.

His strong arms wrapped her tight, pulling her as intimately against him as she could get. He was all hard muscle and she relished the feel of him against her, boldly aroused and taut with desire.

His tongue swirled with hers, evoking a want in her that she'd never experienced before. The hunger she tasted in his mouth clawed inside of her, made her weak and needy in a way that only he could sate.

As the kiss continued, his hands swept first up her

back, then down to cup her buttocks through the silky material of her dress.

His touch filled her with heat. She wanted him in her bedroom, in her bed, his naked body against hers. She wound her arms around his waist beneath the tuxedo jacket and unfastened the cummerbund.

As it fell to the floor, he stepped back from her, his eyes blazing and his chest heaving. "This isn't a good idea." His voice was husky as his gaze swept slowly down the length of her, then back up to meet hers.

His lips might be saying one thing, but the heat of his gaze said quite another. He wanted her. The knowledge torched fire through her, making her think that following through on what they had begun was a very good idea.

"Why not? We're both single and consenting adults." She reached out, took his hand and pulled him out of the office and into her bedroom. He came willingly, although once they were in the bedroom he pulled his hand from hers, his gaze tormented.

"If you don't want me, then I certainly don't want to make you do anything you don't want to," she said, as if it didn't matter to her. But it did. Her heart hammered in her chest. There was no doubt in her mind what she wanted. Him.

"I want you," he replied, his voice thick. He took a step toward her. "I haven't been able to think about much of anything else except how much I want you."

His words made her heart beat faster. He took

another step that brought him to within inches of her. He reached out and ran his fingers through her hair, as if unable to stop himself. "I definitely want you."

"Then what's stopping you?" She felt his hesitation and it was killing her.

He dropped his hand, his eyes darkening with the shadows that often filled them. "Because if we're going to do this, then you have to understand that it isn't any kind of a commitment on my part. This isn't a promise of a relationship, it doesn't mean we owe each other anything."

"And you tell me that I talk too much," she said teasingly.

His cheeks flushed slightly with color and he smiled back at her. "I just want things to be completely clear between us. I don't want there to be any kind of misunderstandings on either side."

"What makes you think I want anything else from you except a hot roll in the hay? Joshua, why don't you just shut up now and kiss me," she demanded.

His eyes flared and he did. It was as if the brief conversation had unleashed something wild inside him. Still kissing her he shrugged out of the tuxedo jacket and removed his shoulder holster and gun.

He then once again wrapped her in his arms and as his fingers worked to lower the zipper at the back of her dress, hers unfastened his shirt buttons.

She wanted to feel the expanse of muscled chest that had taunted her since she'd seen it naked when he'd been on his way to the shower. She wanted to curl her fingers into the dark springy hair that decorated the center of his broad chest.

When her dress zipper was lowered, he slid the garment off her shoulders and it fell to the floor, leaving her clad in her bra, her pantyhose and panties.

He ripped the tie from around his neck and finished unbuttoning his shirt. He shrugged it off, exposing the naked chest that had caused so many fantasies in her mind.

He grabbed his wallet from his back pocket and removed a foil wrapper. He placed it on the nightstand, then reached for her once again.

Within seconds the rest of their clothes quickly joined her dress on the floor and when they were both naked, they fell together on the double bed, a tangle of arms and legs and hunger.

As his mouth took possession of hers, his hands covered her breasts, filling her with a heat that burned all thought from her head.

His mouth left hers and trailed down her neck and across her collarbone, causing sweet sensations of pleasure to shiver through her. She raked her hands down his warm, smooth back, loving the play of muscles beneath the skin.

The golden dusk of twilight filtered through her bedroom curtains and played on his features with a soft illumination. He raised his head to look at her, his eyes gleaming with a breathtaking intensity.

Her heart thundered and desire crashed inside her

as he dipped his head and took one of her nipples in his mouth. She gripped the back of his head, his hair thick and soft beneath her fingers.

Mindless pleasure swept through her as he nipped and licked at her breast and she wanted to give him the same kind of mindless pleasure.

She ran her hand down the hard expanse of his chest, over the washboard muscles of his stomach then curled her fingers around the hard length of him. He moaned, a deep low growl that only increased her need for him.

For the next few minutes they explored each other's body, touching and tasting as the tension in Savannah spiked higher and higher.

It seemed that he could indulge in the foreplay forever, but it didn't take long for her to feel as if she might explode if he didn't take her completely.

"Joshua," she moaned his name. "Make love to me."

He turned over on his side and grabbed the condom from the nightstand. She took it from him, ripped open the package then rolled it onto him. By the time she was finished, he was trembling with his own need.

As he moved on top of her, she opened her legs to welcome him. He entered her, filling her up and at the same time his mouth took hers in a breathless kiss.

For a long moment neither of them moved. He ended the kiss and held her gaze as he moved his hips, withdrawing slightly, then stroking back into her.

The primitive yearning that had possessed her during their foreplay now exploded into something bigger, something so intense she felt as if at any moment she might fragment into a million little pieces.

She met his hips thrust for thrust in a rhythm that grew more frenzied. Her senses were filled with him, his scent, his touch and the sound of his rapid breaths and low moans. His features were taut, lips pulled tight and eyes smoky as he moved faster and faster.

Her release crashed through her and she clung to him, half-crying, half-laughing as waves of sensation washed over her. It was as if he'd only waited for her before allowing himself to let go. He stiffened against her, crying out her name as he shuddered, then collapsed on top of her.

As they waited for normal breathing to resume, for heartbeats to slow, she stroked her hands down his back, loving the feel of his warm skin. She was grateful he didn't immediately jump out of the bed, eager to be away from her now that they'd sated themselves.

He finally rolled to her side, but gathered her in his arms. "That was amazing," he said.

She smiled and placed her hand on the side of his face where she could feel the faint stubble of whiskers. "I think I've wanted to do this from the minute you took off your shirt and offered to scrub my back in your shower."

He didn't give her a responding smile, but instead

a frown furrowed his forehead. She could almost see the wheels turning in his head and she sighed impatiently. "Honestly, Joshua, if you're worried that somehow I'm going to get all mushy and romantic on you, don't."

A flash of relief shone from his eyes. She propped herself up on one elbow, vaguely irritated. "Other women might think you're all that, but this was just a hormone call as far as I'm concerned."

He propped himself up on his elbow, his face mere inches from hers. "Do you get these hormone calls often?"

She knew he was really asking about past relationships. "It's been over a year since I've been with anyone."

"Why is that?" He reached out and swept a curl away from her eyes.

He confused her. He'd been so intent in making sure she understood this meant nothing to him. Yet he was exhibiting a gentleness that pulled her toward him and a curiosity about her that seemed in direct conflict to his earlier words.

"I don't know. Relationships aren't a priority for me." There was no way she intended to confess to him that relationships had always been difficult for her, that she'd never found a man who loved her, flaws and all. "What about you? Did you leave a trail of broken hearts back in New York?"

"Not me. I tried to make sure hearts didn't get involved."

Somehow that didn't surprise her. "It must have been rough growing up without a mother," she said, changing the subject.

The shadows that had momentarily drifted across his eyes lifted and he shrugged. "It's hard to miss what you never knew. I was just a baby when she was killed. I have no memories of her at all."

"And they never found out who killed her?"

"I think it's the only unsolved homicide that's ever happened in Cotter Creek," he replied.

"Sometimes I wish I had less memories of my mother," she said drily.

"I gather from little things you've said about her that she was difficult."

She smiled ruefully. "There are some people who are just not cut out to be parents. My mother and father were two of those people. Sometimes I think it would have been easier to be raised by a pack of wolves."

"Is that why you left Scottsdale?"

"I left because it was time for me to leave. It was time for me to figure out who I was separate from my parents." Funny, they'd spent the entire week together but this was the first real conversation of substance they'd shared.

"I can understand that." Once again a darkness filled his eyes. "That was why I decided to head to New York, because I needed to know who I was aside from being a member of the West family."

She wanted to ask him more, wanted to know

about the thoughts that caused those shadows, but knew she had no right. This night was supposed to mean nothing and that meant she had no ownership of his inner thoughts.

"When are you going to let me interview you for my column?" she asked.

He grinned. "You never give up, do you?"

She curled her fingers into his chest hair. "I just think you'd be an interesting subject."

"Trust me, it would be the most boring interview you've ever conducted."

She sighed. "So, what happens now in our investigation?"

He sat up and swiped a hand through his hair. "We need to find out what happened to the land, if it was sold, if it went to heirs, whatever."

"What made you think of it? How did you put it all together?" She sat up, too, clutching the sheet to her chest.

"Sheila Wadsworth. I had a brief conversation with her at the reception and something just clicked in my head." He swung his legs over the side of the bed and reached for his slacks. "I'll be right back." He held his pants in front of him as he left the room and a moment later she heard the click of the bathroom door.

She lay back against her pillow and closed her eyes, for a moment allowing herself to replay each and every kiss, each and every caress they had shared. It had been more than amazing. And it didn't mean anything. She couldn't allow it to mean anything.

You'd better get used to being alone, Savannah Marie. You don't have many assets to offer a man.

"Thanks, Mother," Savannah said softly and forcefully shoved her mother's words to the back of her head. She suddenly remembered Joshua's words when they had arrived at the wedding.

He'd said that somebody had done a number on her. Of course, he was right. For as long as she could remember, her mother had pointed out all her flaws, both physical and character ones.

The main reason Savannah had left Scottsdale was to figure out who she was and what she had to offer to other people without the constant negativity from her parents. She'd needed to get away from the constant hurt that her parents could inflict on her.

She opened her eyes as she heard the bathroom door open. Joshua came back into the bedroom clad in his slacks. "You want to get dressed and I'll take you back to the party?" he asked as he grabbed his shirt from the floor. "It will probably go on until the wee hours of the morning."

There was a part of her that wanted to go back to the party. It would be fun to get Joshua out on the dance floor with her, fun to drink too much champagne and laugh with him. But, there was another part of her that wanted to remain in the bed that smelled of him, that retained his warmth.

"No, I think I'll stay right here," she replied. She

wanted to just stay in bed and savor the memory of their lovemaking. "Besides, I imagine it won't be long before Winnie gets home."

"What are your plans for tomorrow?" He fastened his cummerbund around his waist, then reached for the bow tie.

"Most Sundays I just hang around here. Take the day off, Joshua." Once again she sat up. "In fact, I was going to talk to you about this bodyguarding business. Nothing has happened to make us think I'm in any danger since that shooting at the newspaper office. Maybe that really didn't have anything to do with me. Maybe you playing bodyguard is just a waste of your time."

He frowned and put on his holster. "Next week we're going to start asking some questions that might make somebody uncomfortable. I'd feel better if we just leave things the way they are for now, at least until we know more about what's going on."

She wasn't sure why, but she was pleased that he didn't want to take the easy out that she had offered him. Although she certainly wasn't going to get all silly over him, she was glad to have him by her side.

"You know, Sheila Wadsworth has been not-so-subtly indicating to me that she would love to be interviewed for my column. Maybe I should call her tomorrow and set up a time for Monday. If anyone knows who owns those places now, she'd know."

"Great idea. You have a piece of paper and a pen? I'm going to be in and out tomorrow and I'll give you my cell phone number and you can call and let me know what you've set up for Monday."

She reached into her nightstand and pulled out a small notepad and pen. He took them from her, wrote his number, then placed it on the nightstand. He grabbed his shoulder holster and gun and put them on, then pulled on his tux jacket. "Sure you don't want to go back to the reception?"

She snuggled back beneath the sheets. "Sure you don't want to stay here?"

His eyes flashed with heat. "Don't tempt me."

Oh, but she wanted to tempt him. She'd love nothing more than to invite him back into her bed and make love with him until the sun came up in the morning. But, her desire for that frightened her just a little bit.

"Get back to the party and I'll call you tomorrow," she said.

When he left he seemed to take all the energy in the room with him. Night was falling outside the window and she almost wished she'd gotten up and returned to the party with him.

She could imagine the tent lit against the darkness, laughter spilling out as the band played and people danced and celebrated the joy of Clay and Libby's union. But, making love with Joshua had shaken her up more than she cared to admit.

By nature she was cautious, especially when it came to sex. Jumping into bed with Joshua after knowing him only a little over a week had definitely

been out of character for her. But, the enforced closeness that they had shared over the past week and a
half had built up not only an intense desire but also
a strange sense of intimacy.

She rolled over on her side as a small wave of
irritation niggled at her. It was definitely egotisti-
cal of him to worry that somehow by going to bed
with her she'd expect something more from him.
Why didn't he worry about wanting something
more from her?

He was probably accustomed to women
throwing themselves at him, but she didn't intend
to be one of the lovesick masses who wished Joshua
West could commit.

She sighed and closed her eyes and within
minutes fell into a deep, dreamless sleep.

She had no idea what awakened her, whether it
was a noise in the room or something else. But, the
moment sleep fell away she sensed that she was no
longer alone in the room.

Suddenly the blanket was yanked over her head
and a weight fell on top of her. Any fogginess of
residual sleep fell away. Claustrophobia closed her
throat as she fought to be released from the cocoon
of blankets that held her captive.

"Hey," she cried, wondering if Joshua had
returned and was playing some kind of a sick joke
on her. "This isn't funny."

Her heart hammered as she increased her efforts
to get free. Whoever held the blankets held them

tight, keeping her captive and unable to see what was going on. "Let me up," she cried, kicking her feet and flailing her arms in an effort to get free.

The first blow caught her in the stomach, a vicious punch that knocked the air from her lungs and assured her that whatever was happening certainly wasn't a joke.

Frantically she kicked out and fought, her throat closing as terror possessed her. As terrifying as the blow to her midsection had been, equally as horrifying was her inability to see her attacker.

A second punch to the stomach forced a rising nausea. When another blow struck her hip, she gave up all efforts to get free of the blankets and instead rolled onto her side and pulled herself into a fetal ball in order to protect herself from the blows that rained down on her.

A hit to her jaw stunned her and stars swam in her head. Tears filled her eyes as she realized she was about to get beaten to death in her own bed. With a cry of rage, she renewed her fight to free herself from the blankets.

She managed to get a leg free and kicked wildly. She connected with something and heard a sharp moan. Sobbing, she kicked again and again.

"Savannah. Are you home, dear?" Winnie's voice came from the downstairs.

Savannah froze. Oh, God. No. Fear for her elderly landlady sizzled through her. "Winnie! Run! Run, Winnie," she screamed.

As she frantically fought the blankets, she heard the thud of footsteps racing down the stairs, then Winnie's high-pitched scream.

Chapter 9

It had been a huge mistake. As Joshua drove back toward the West ranch, the weight of his mistake hung heavy in his heart.

He'd been on a slow simmer where Savannah was concerned. He had no idea why she'd affected him so intensely, but someplace in the back of his mind he'd hoped that by sating his desire for her once, it would be done and over.

Unfortunately, it hadn't worked out that way. Rather than being done, just thinking about what they'd just shared made him want to share it again. He'd been so tempted to forget returning to the reception and instead crawl back into bed with her.

At least he didn't have to worry about her getting

emotionally involved. She seemed less inclined to form a commitment with anyone than he did.

In fact, she'd made it pretty clear to him that he'd been nothing but a booty call. It was an odd feeling for him and one he was surprised to discover didn't feel altogether terrific.

He tightened his grip on the steering wheel as if symbolically getting a grip on himself. Despite the fact that the sex with Savannah had been unbelievably hot, in spite of the fact that she could make him laugh and at times pulled forth a protectiveness inside him, he wasn't looking for any kind of a real hookup at this point in his life.

Still, the thought of Savannah's warm curves in his arms, the fire that had been in her kiss and her total giving to him as they'd made love couldn't easily be dismissed from his mind.

He was halfway between the ranch and town when he saw the sheriff's car racing toward him, the cherry light on top flashing against the darkness of the night.

Most everyone in town was at the West ranch. Where could Jim be heading? With an odd, sick premonition, Joshua flashed his lights a couple of times and Ramsey pulled to a halt next to Joshua's truck.

He rolled down his window and Joshua did the same. "Something happened at Winnie Halifax's place," he said.

The premonition exploded into fear. "I just left there a few minutes ago," Joshua said. "What happened?"

"Apparently somebody attacked the women."

The words were scarcely out of Ramsey's mouth before Joshua pulled a U-turn and roared back the way he'd come. He was vaguely conscious of the lights of the sheriff's car following close behind as he sped back to Winnie's.

Somebody attacked the women. Somebody attacked the women. The words played and replayed in his head in a sick echo.

What exactly had happened? How badly was she hurt? Dammit, he should have never left her alone. What in the hell had he been thinking, and who had made the call to Jim? He held the steering wheel so tightly he felt as if his fingers might break.

How had they gotten inside the house? He'd locked the front door when he'd left Winnie's, knowing Savannah was still snuggled down in bed. Had the attacker broken in or had Savannah let somebody in?

Savannah might have opened the door to an attractive woman, not knowing the danger. Lauren could charm her way past a palace guard if she wanted inside badly enough.

He should have told somebody about Lauren. He should have swallowed his pride and told his family, told Savannah about the danger Lauren might pose.

Attacked. Dammit, what did that mean? Had she been raped? Stabbed? Shot? Had Winnie gotten home and found Savannah dead in her bed? Was Savannah lying in a pool of her own blood as Winnie had frantically called the sheriff?

"Jesus," he whispered. Emotion clawed up his throat as he pulled to a halt in front of the Halifax two-story house.

It looked as if every light in the house was on. Joshua pulled his gun as he left the truck and raced toward the front door.

He burst inside and nearly fell to his knees in relief as he saw Winnie and Savannah sitting on the sofa, their arms wound around each other. Whatever had happened, at least they were both alive.

"Joshua." Savannah stood and launched herself into his arms as deep, wrenching sobs shook her body. She wore a thin blue cotton robe and as he held her, he was aware that she had nothing on beneath it. But, more importantly, she was wonderfully alive in his arms.

Her tears only lasted a minute, then she stepped back from him and wiped her cheeks. Joshua's stomach knotted as he noticed for the first time the redness of her lower jaw. He reached out and gently touched the spot. "What happened?" he asked.

At that moment Ramsey flew through the door.

Savannah resumed her seat next to Winnie, who looked shaken and frail. "After you left, I decided to go to bed," Savannah said with a meaningful glance at him. She obviously didn't want them to know that the two of them had been in bed together and that's where Joshua had left her.

She crossed her arms in front of her chest and hugged herself. "I fell asleep and the next thing I knew somebody was on top of me, punching me.

Whoever it was had me trapped beneath the blankets and they kept hitting me."

Her terror radiated from her eyes and Joshua wanted to hit somebody, punish whoever was responsible for that fear, for her pain. "They kept hitting me and hitting me and I couldn't get free of the covers."

She reached up and touched her jaw and winced slightly. "I think they would have beaten me to death if Winnie hadn't arrived home when she did." She grabbed the older woman's hand.

"I unlocked the front door and stepped inside," Winnie said, her voice faint and trembling. "Then I called up to Savannah. The next thing I knew somebody came crashing down the stairs, knocked me clear over and flew out the front door."

"Did you get a look at the intruder?" Ramsey asked.

Winnie shook her head, her pale blue eyes filling with tears. "It all happened so fast. I wasn't expecting it. Whoever it was had on all black and maybe a ski mask. All I saw was black, then I was on the floor and he was gone."

Joshua had an incredible need to pull Savannah back into his arms, to assure himself that she was really all right. He told himself the need had nothing to do with her as a person but rather because he was supposed to protect her, and he'd failed.

"I'm going to take a look outside," Jim said.

"I'll look around in here and see if I can tell how

they got inside," Joshua replied. Jim nodded and the men parted ways, leaving Winnie and Savannah seated side-by-side on the sofa.

It took him only a step into the kitchen to see how the intruder had gained access to the house. The window beside the kitchen table was broken, the screen torn away to provide an easy entry.

Cold rage swept over him as he thought of Savannah's reddened jaw, how she'd been trapped in the blankets while somebody had pummeled her. What would have happened had Winnie not come home when she had? The thought sent a new wave of rage through him.

Had it been Lauren? Certainly he suspected she was capable of such an attack. At one time he'd believed he was a good judge of character, but his experience with Lauren had shaken that belief right out of him.

He left the kitchen and checked the rest of the house. He touched nothing in Savannah's bedroom, but looked for clues as to the identity of the intruder. Unfortunately, if the person had worn a ski mask, the odds of finding a hair or any other evidence were minimal.

Sheriff Ramsey joined him in the bedroom, a frown tugging his graying eyebrows together. "I didn't see anything outside. Saw the window in the kitchen so I guess we know how they got inside." He looked around the room in obvious frustration. "Who in the hell would do such a thing?"

"That's what I was just asking myself. It's the craziest thing I've ever heard."

Joshua stood by the door while Ramsey wandered around the room, obviously looking for the same things Joshua had looked for…clues as to who might have been in the room beating up Savannah.

"I don't think you'll find anything useful," Joshua said. "If what Savannah and Winnie believe is true, that the perp was wearing all black and a ski mask, then I imagine he or she was also wearing gloves."

"I think you're probably right," Sheriff Ramsey agreed. He looked at Joshua in speculation. "You think this has something to do with all the questions Savannah has been asking around town?"

"I think anything is possible." He told Sheriff Ramsey the latest information he and Savannah had come up with as to the location of the land and the coinciding accidental deaths. With each word he spoke, Jim Ramsey's frown grew increasingly deeper.

"I'd like us to work together on this, Joshua. I want to get to the bottom of this as quickly as possible."

Joshua nodded. "I think she's right, Jim. I think there's something going on here."

A hard light gleamed from Ramsey's eyes. "Until I decide to retire, this is still my town and I'll be damned if I'll just sit by and allow some sort of criminal activity to take place right under my nose. I'm going to take statements from the women, then go get my fingerprint kit and see what I can find.

Who knows, maybe we'll get lucky and the perp left a print behind."

While Jim took down the official statements, Joshua went out to Winnie's garage and found a piece of plywood to temporarily cover the broken kitchen window.

It was after eleven when Jim finally left the house. "I'm going to bed," Winnie said. "It's been a trying night and I'm exhausted." She got up from the sofa, her weariness evident in her sagging shoulders.

Savannah stood as well and gave the woman a hug. "I'm so sorry, Winnie."

"You don't have anything to be sorry about, child."

"Are you sure you're all right?" Savannah asked.

Winnie smiled tiredly. "I'm fine, dear. It takes a lot more than a masked man to get me down."

As Winnie went down the hallway toward the bedroom, Savannah looked at Joshua, her eyes still retaining the fear of what she'd experienced. Never had a woman looked as if she needed a hug as much as Savannah did at that moment.

But, before he could decide if that was a good idea or not, she seemed to find some source of inner strength. She straightened her shoulders, tilted her chin up and smiled.

"Well, this has been interesting. How about I make some coffee and we talk about it," she said.

Nothing she had done or said over the past week earned as much of his respect as she did at that moment. With her eyes shining overly bright and her lower lip trembling slightly, she nevertheless displayed a core of strength he couldn't help but admire.

"Coffee sounds great," he said. He had a feeling she wasn't ready for him to leave, but she couldn't know he didn't intend to go anywhere, at least not until after he told her about Lauren. She had a right to know what his past might have brought into her life.

He sat at the table and watched silently as she busied herself making a short pot of coffee. When it began to drip into the glass carafe, she turned and looked at him, her eyes less haunted than they'd been moments before.

"The redness in your jaw is fading," he observed. "I don't think you're going to bruise."

She reached up and touched the spot, then dropped her arm to her side. "I've got to tell you, even though the attack lasted only a couple of minutes, they were the scariest minutes of my life. At first I thought maybe it was you, that you'd decided to come back. When the covers were pulled up over my head, I thought you were playing some sort of a joke on me."

Again a fierce protectiveness filled Joshua, along with a healthy dose of anger. "I'm sorry, Savannah. I'm sorry I left you alone and vulnerable."

"It's not your fault." Her eyes darkened as she looked at the board covering the broken window.

"You think you're safe locked in your own home, then something like this happens and it shakes up any sense of safety you have."

She turned back to the coffeepot and poured them each a cup of the fresh brew. She set his cup in front of him, then joined him at the table and curled her fingers around her cup. "I guess I should be grateful that Winnie arrived home when she did and that whoever attacked me used fists instead of a knife."

The visual picture of her trapped in the sheets while somebody stabbed her over and over caused Joshua's heart to stutter in his chest. This night could have ended so differently. It could have ended in tragedy.

"Could you tell if your attacker was a male or female?" he asked.

She sat back in her chair and looked at him in surprise. "I just assumed it was a man." She frowned thoughtfully. "Why would you think it might have been a woman?"

He took a sip of his coffee, then drew a deep breath. "You asked me after the night of the shooting who I might have pissed off since returning home to Cotter Creek. As far as I know I haven't made anyone mad since I've been back home, but I left somebody in New York who would love to hurt me and whoever she thinks I might care about."

Savannah's frown deepened. "And you think that person might have come here to Cotter Creek? That she might be the one who attacked me tonight? My

God, Joshua, what did you do to her to inspire such hatred?"

He sighed. *Failure*, a little voice whispered in his head. "Her name is Lauren Edwards. I met her at a club one night. She was gorgeous and smart. She told me she worked at a law firm as a paralegal and was considering going to law school to become an attorney."

He scooted his chair back and stood, too restless to sit as he thought of how badly he'd screwed up. "Anyway, we hooked up that first night and I thought we were both on the same page. I thought she understood that I wasn't looking for anything permanent. I thought we were both wanting the same things, just a little bit of fun and nothing serious."

"But she wanted more?"

"Apparently." He began to pace the small confines of the kitchen, his mind going back over the last couple of weeks he'd spent in New York. "Anyway, we saw each other for about a month and I thought everything was cool. We hadn't talked about an exclusive relationship. Hell, we hadn't talked about a relationship at all. We weren't seeing each other on any regular basis."

"But she thought of it as something more than it was?" Savannah asked.

"She started planning a wedding and that's when I called a halt to things. I tried to be nice and let her down gently, but I sure as hell wasn't prepared to marry her after a month."

"I'm guessing she took it badly?"

"That's an understatement. A couple of nights after I broke it off with her, I met a female coworker for dinner. We were in the middle of our meal when Lauren burst into the restaurant like some crazy person."

He stopped his pacing and leaned with his back against the refrigerator. That night had been the most embarrassing that Joshua had ever experienced in his life. "She came in screaming about how I'd betrayed her. She called the woman I was with a slut and tried to fight her. She was escorted out of the restaurant, but when my coworker went to leave, she discovered that the windows in her car had all been broken out."

He began to pace again. "Then the next day while I was at work, my apartment was broken into." He still remembered the stunned shock he'd felt when he'd stepped into his apartment. "Everything was destroyed, slashed with a knife, smashed beyond repair. It took a tremendous amount of rage to do the kind of damage that was done."

"She wasn't arrested?" A tiny frown raced across Savannah's forehead.

"I knew she did it. The police questioned her, but unfortunately one of her girlfriends provided an alibi."

"And you think maybe this Lauren followed you here? That she might have been the person who tried to beat me up tonight?"

He returned to the table before answering. "I think it's possible," he said. "I've been trying to get in touch with Lauren ever since the night of the shooting, but she's not answering her home phone. I couldn't remember what law firm she worked for, but I finally got a hold of a mutual friend who told me. The receptionist at the law firm where she worked said she'd taken some vacation time, but I don't know if she's still in New York or not."

"Isn't there somebody you can call to see if she's still in town?" Savannah asked.

"I tried. I spoke with several of our mutual friends and nobody has seen her for the past week or so."

"But that doesn't mean she isn't still in New York."

Joshua shrugged. "True. But I figured it was best I tell you about her, just in case."

"So, basically I should watch my back for a love-crazed New Yorker who has claimed you as her man."

The lightness of her tone irritated him. Didn't she understand that he'd somehow screwed up? That he'd misjudged the entire situation?

"It's not funny," he said with a scowl. "I don't know what this woman is capable of, I don't know how dangerous she might be."

Her eyes darkened once again and one slender hand reached up to touch her jaw. "I guess she's dangerous enough if she's the one who attacked me tonight." She finished her coffee, then got up and carried her cup to the sink.

She rinsed out the cup then turned to face him.

"I'll keep an eye out for women I don't know, but you realize it's equally as possible that whoever attacked me tonight did so because we're making somebody nervous with all our questions about those deaths."

"How many people have you talked to about your suspicions?" he asked.

Her cheeks pinkened slightly. "You should know by now I like to talk. I told anyone and everyone who would listen that I thought something bad was happening. I talked to waitresses and sales clerks, the mayor and members of the city council."

He also took his cup to the sink, rinsed it then turned to her. She looked tired and although her jaw wasn't as red as it had been, it still held a touch of color. He reached out and placed his fingers against the redness. "Are you sure you're all right? Were you hurt anywhere else?"

She leaned toward him as if to welcome his touch. "I took a punch to the stomach and a few to the back, but I'm okay. I was terrified when it was happening, but the moment you walked in here I knew it was all going to be okay."

Her words both touched and concerned him. He didn't want her depending on him. He obviously didn't have the tools to judge people and their intentions, which was an integral part of being in the personal protection business.

He dropped his hand from her face and stepped back, needing to distance himself from her. "We just need to be smart and understand that for whatever reason you're at risk."

She nodded and wrapped her arms around herself. She looked small and vulnerable. "I'm sorry you missed the rest of the party."

He smiled. "There will be other parties. You need to go to bed. It's late."

"And I'm beyond exhausted." She glanced over to the boarded-up window, then back at him, her gaze holding a dark whisper of fear. "You don't think the attacker will come back again tonight, do you?"

"If it would make you feel better, I'll sleep here on the sofa for tonight."

"I hate to ask you to do that, but it would make me feel better." She flashed a tight smile. "I'll bet you're sorry you ever got involved in all this," she said as they left the kitchen.

"If it's Lauren, then I'm sorry I got you involved," he replied. It had been easier to tell her about Lauren than he'd thought it would be. In fact, he had a feeling he could talk to Savannah about anything.

"I'll just get you a pillow and some blankets," she said as they moved into the living room. She disappeared down the hallway and returned a moment later with the bedding in her arms. "Are you sure you don't mind staying here?" Her brow wrinkled with worry.

"It's fine," he reassured her. "I wouldn't have offered if I minded." He took the bedding from her arms. "Now, you'd better get some sleep."

She reached up on her tiptoes and kissed his cheek. The imprint of her lips shot heat straight to his heart. He backed away from her, confused by his reaction, vaguely irritated by a quick whip of desire that swept through him.

"Goodnight, Joshua." She walked to the stairway but before she took a step up she turned back to look at him. "The thing with Lauren, at least you know you managed to inspire tremendous passion in somebody. That's something I don't expect to do in my lifetime." She didn't wait for his reply, but instead climbed the stairs.

He watched her until she disappeared from his sight, then he unfolded the blankets and made his bed for the night on the sofa. Whatever he'd inspired in Lauren, he didn't believe it had anything to do with real passion. It had everything to do with sick obsession.

As he placed his gun on the coffee table in easy reach, he thought of what she'd said about his being sorry he'd gotten involved.

The truth was he felt more alive, more vital than he had since he'd left Cotter Creek almost one and a half years before. The problem was he didn't know if it was the woman or the potential danger that had his blood pumping and his adrenaline flowing.

Chapter 10

"Don't forget the security code if you get home before me this afternoon," Winnie said over breakfast Monday morning. "I'm having my hair and nails done today."

Winnie had arranged for a security system to be installed the day before, insisting that she should have done it years ago when her husband had first passed away and left her all alone.

Savannah had to confess, the new alarm system definitely gave her a sense of security that had been stripped from her with the attack. "I won't be home until later this evening. First thing this morning Joshua and I are heading to City Hall to see Lillian. We want to find out who owns the property of the ranchers who died. Then, I have an early dinner date with Sheila Wadsworth."

Winnie wrinkled her nose. "Now that's a woman who doesn't know the meaning of subtle."

Savannah laughed, thinking of Sheila's penchant for glitter and sequins. "She certainly hasn't been subtle about wanting me to interview her for my column."

"Sheila will do almost anything for attention or money," Winnie said. "She's been like that all her life. Rumor has it that she met her husband when she joined some dating service. Of course, I try not to listen to rumor." Winnie smiled slyly.

Once again Savannah laughed and carried her breakfast dishes to the sink. "This town runs on gossip. It's the favorite pasttime of everyone."

Winnie's smile increased. "And I know the latest piece of gossip that's making the rounds."

Savannah rinsed off her dishes, placed them in the dishwasher, then turned and looked at her landlady. "And what would that be?"

"Everyone is talking about how quickly you managed to snap up the most eligible bachelor in town."

"I didn't snap him up. We're just working together, that's all," Savannah exclaimed, her cheeks warming with a blush.

Winnie raised an eyebrow. "You two might just be working together, but that doesn't account for the sparks that fly in the air whenever the two of you are in the same room."

"Nonsense," Savannah scoffed as she felt her blush deepen, spilling heat into her cheeks. "There is absolutely nothing personal going on between Joshua and me."

Except she hadn't been able to forget what it felt like to be held in his arms, to be kissed with his lips, to feel his body taking hers. "And speaking of Joshua, he should be here anytime. I'm going to run upstairs and grab my purse and notebook."

Alone in her room, she sat on the edge of the bed and thought about what Winnie had said. If there were any sparks in the air between her and Joshua it was only because of the physical attraction she felt for him and nothing else.

It had been almost impossible for her to fall asleep Saturday night knowing he was downstairs on the sofa. She'd wanted nothing more than to go downstairs and get him and bring him into her bed.

She'd wanted his strong, warm arms holding her through the remainder of the night. Her desire was so intense it had frightened her. She told herself it was because of the trauma she'd suffered, but she suspected it was something deeper and more profound than that.

He'd left the next morning after the alarm system had been installed and they had only spoken on the phone once during the day to set up a time for him to pick her up this morning.

Despite that she had known him less than two weeks, in spite of the fact that they'd made love only once, he was getting beneath her defenses, making her wish for things she'd never wished for before.

"Savannah Marie, get a hold of yourself," she said aloud. She had sworn to Joshua that she wasn't going to get all mushy and romantic where he was concerned and she was determined to keep her word.

She grabbed her purse and notebook and left the bedroom. She'd just hit the bottom of the stairs when the doorbell rang.

It was Joshua. She tried to ignore the expanse of her heart at the sight of him. Clad in a pair of jeans, with a blue and gray sports shirt and dark gray sports coat, he threatened to take her breath away.

"All set?" he asked.

She nodded. "Winnie, we're leaving," she yelled toward the kitchen.

Within minutes Savannah and Joshua were in his truck and headed toward City Hall. She drew a deep breath, enjoying the scent of him, that wonderful blend of sunshine and clean male.

"What happens if we don't see anything suspicious about the sale of those properties?" she asked.

"Then I guess you just have to suffer through an interview with Sheila and write a column about her." He flashed a quick glance at her, his eyes lit with humor.

She smiled. "I guess that's not the worst thing in the world. So, what did you do on your day off yesterday?"

"I moved."

She looked at him in surprise. "You moved? Where?"

"There's a little two-bedroom cottage down the lane from the big house. It used to be used by a variety of ranch managers, but for the past several years Zack lived there. Since he and Katie got married, the place has been empty."

"Is there a reason for the move?" She couldn't imagine leaving the love and support that brimmed to the top at the West ranch for isolation in a cabin.

He hesitated a long moment before answering. "I just got used to being alone in New York and prefer to be by myself."

She didn't believe him. There was something more to it than that. It surprised her how much she wanted to know everything about him, all his thoughts, his worries, his dreams.

She told herself it was only because she was a reporter and he was an intriguing man from a powerful family, but she knew she was only fooling herself. She was beginning to care about Joshua West, and that scared the hell out of her.

Maybe she was just feeling unusually emotional because of the attack and it was only natural she'd turn to Joshua for comfort and support. She had nobody else to turn to.

A wave of loneliness suddenly overtook her. She had parents who had never really bonded with her, a friend who had either committed suicide or been murdered and a man who had slept with her but had made it clear he wanted nothing more from her than a booty call. If she thought about it for too long she'd get downright depressed.

"It's not like you to be so quiet," he observed, breaking into her somber thoughts.

"Are you implying that I normally talk your ear off?"

He grinned. "Yeah, that's pretty much what I'm saying." He pulled into a parking place in front of the brick one-story city hall. He cut the engine, then turned to face her, the smile gone. "Are you okay? Did you sleep all right last night?"

"I slept fine," she assured him. "It's amazing how much a little thing like a state-of-the-art alarm system can do for your peace of mind." She unfastened her seat belt. "And now let's go inside and see how many cages we can rattle today."

She'd just stepped out of the truck when a male voice called her name. She whirled around to see Larry Davidson hurrying toward her. She smiled at the rugged cowhand who wore his black hat at a jaunty angle.

"Hi, Larry. How's life treating you?"

"Not bad." He shot a glance at Joshua.

"Do you two know each other?" She looked from Joshua to Larry.

"Haven't had the pleasure," Larry said and held out a hand.

The men made their introductions, then Larry

faced Savannah once again. "Could I talk to you alone for a moment?" he asked.

"I'll wait right over there," Joshua said and walked several feet away.

Larry swept his hat off his head, revealing a head of unruly dark blond hair. He worried the brim of his hat between his thick callused fingers. "I was just wondering if maybe you'd like to have dinner with me sometime."

Savannah took a step back from him, surprised by the invitation. Perhaps if she hadn't met Joshua she might have considered accepting his offer. But it didn't seem right to sleep with one man and have dinner with another. Besides, there was absolutely no sparks where Larry was concerned.

"Thanks, Larry, but right now I'm really busy with work." He looked crestfallen. "Maybe you could check back with me in a couple of weeks," she added, not wanting to hurt his feelings.

"I'll do that," he said and plopped his hat back on his head, then turned and headed down the sidewalk.

Savannah rejoined Joshua, who stood near the front door of the city hall building. He scowled. "How do you know that guy?"

"One of the first people I profiled when I started my column was Mayor Sharp. Larry works on the Mayor's ranch, and while I was out there he showed me around the place."

"What did he want?" The scowl showed no sign of lifting.

"He wanted to ask me out to dinner," she said, then added, "not that it's any of your business."

"I hope you turned him down. He's definitely not your type."

She looked at him in surprise. "And just what is my type?"

The scowl finally vanished, replaced by a knowing glint in his eyes. "He has to be strong, otherwise you'd ride ripshod all over him. And he has to have money." His gaze slowly slid down the length of her. "Because you are definitely a high maintenance kind of woman."

"I have my own money, thank you very much," she replied.

"Oh, and he'll have to be the silent type because the odds are good he'll rarely get a word in edgewise."

"Ha, ha, I bet you think you're funny." She grabbed him by the arm and steered him toward the door. "Come on, let's see if you can exude some of that Joshua charm on Lillian so she won't take all day getting the records we want to see."

Cotter Creek City Hall was a study in opulence for a Midwest cow town. The floor was imported gray marble with pale pink veins, more befitting a plush hotel than a government building.

Several years ago Aaron Sharp had pushed for major renovations for City Hall, resulting in mahogany counters, gleaming brass fixtures and the latest in computer technology.

One thing that hadn't changed was Lillian. She

sat at a desk behind the counter, the same place she had sat five days a week for the past ten years.

She got up from her desk as they came in, a smile of welcome on her wrinkled face. "You must not be here to pay taxes because you don't look mad."

"Actually, we're here for some information," Savannah said. "We'd like to find out who owns some of the property in the area."

"Should be easy enough," Lillian said. She took the list of properties that Savannah had prepared. "It's going to take me a few minutes."

"We'll wait," Joshua said.

As Lillian returned to her desk and her computer, Savannah tried to still her racing heart. She was anxious to find out what information Lillian might be able to give them, but she suspected her quick heartbeat might also be because as crazy as it sounded, Joshua had acted like a jealous suitor for a moment.

She glanced over to where he stood leaning against the counter. *Don't be ridiculous, Savannah Marie. A man who looks like Joshua might sleep with you because you're convenient, but when it comes time for him to settle down, it won't be with a woman like you.*

"Shut up, Mother," Savannah muttered.

"Excuse me?" Joshua eyed her curiously.

"Nothing, I was just talking to myself."

He grinned, that easy, lazy smile that never failed to warm her. "It's nice to know you don't need anyone else around to fulfill your need for meaning-less chatter."

She might have been offended by his words if it hadn't been for a soft, indulgent light that filled the green of his eyes.

"I spent most of my childhood talking to myself," she said lightly. "I'm used to it."

His smile faltered and instead he gazed at her for a long, somber moment. "I'm sorry about that."

There was something soft, something gentle in his voice that pierced through the protective barrier she kept so firmly around her heart. For just a moment as she looked into his eyes hope buoyed inside her, a fragile hope that she was afraid to hang onto. She feared that if she grasped it too tightly, she'd be shattered when she discovered her mother had been right about her after all.

"This is odd," Lillian said as she handed Joshua the information they'd been seeking. "All of those properties are listed to two men who have the same address in Boston. Isn't that odd?" Lillian looked from Joshua to Savannah.

"It's more than odd," Joshua said as he exchanged a meaningful glance with Savannah. "Come on, we've got more work to do."

"I was right, wasn't I, Joshua?" Savannah said as they left City Hall. "This is proof, isn't it?" Her cheeks flushed becomingly. "I knew I wasn't crazy. I might be a lot of things, but I'm not crazy." She followed him down the sidewalk. "Where are we going? What happens now?"

"We're going to see if we can find out who these two men are and why they have the same Boston address. Dalton should be in the office and with his help maybe we can get some answers before your dinner date with Sheila."

A hard knot pressed inside his chest. Savannah had been right. There was something evil happening in the town he loved. Somebody was buying up all the land, land that had belonged to men who had died in what now seemed like damned suspicious accidents.

He'd worried that somehow Lauren had found him and set her sights on Savannah. He'd believed that the attacks on her had been from the woman he'd left behind in New York City. Now he wasn't so sure.

If this was as big as he thought it might be, then it might just be big enough for Savannah's questions to be making somebody very nervous. He fought an impulse to reach out and take her hand in his, as if to assure himself that at least for the moment she was safe.

The Wild West Protective Services wooden sign creaked on its hinges in the midmorning breeze as he and Savannah approached the front door.

Inside Dalton sat at the desk, looking bored and with a computer game pulled up in front of him. "Hey, what's up?" He greeted them and closed down the game.

"We need some answers and I'm hoping you can get them off the Internet," Joshua said. He handed

Dalton the sheet of paper Lillian had printed out for them with the names and addresses of the men who owned the properties.

"I want to know who these men are and why they're buying up land in Cotter Creek," Joshua said, then went on to explain what he and Savannah had been investigating.

"Strange," Dalton said when he'd finished. "Why would a couple of Boston men want anything to do with Cotter Creek?"

"That's what I'm hoping you can find out," Joshua replied.

"This may take a little while," Dalton said.

Joshua looked at Savannah. "Want to grab a quick cup of coffee at the café while we wait?"

"Sounds good to me," she replied.

"We'll be back in twenty minutes or so," Joshua said to his brother, who nodded absently, his attention totally focused on his task.

There was no way Joshua felt like just sitting and waiting in the office. He knew Dalton would work better if he didn't have the distraction of him and Savannah standing over him.

"What does all this mean, Joshua?" Savannah asked him a few minutes later as they sat at a back booth in the café. "Why would those men be buying land here?"

"I don't know. Maybe Dalton will come up with some answers that will make sense."

She frowned thoughtfully. "You think those men

are responsible for all those ranchers' deaths? Do you think one of those men killed Charlie?"

"Who knows? To be perfectly honest, I don't know what to think." He took a sip of the strong, hot coffee, then continued. "Cotter Creek is such a small town. I do find it difficult to believe that there are strangers running around killing people then buying up their land. People around here notice strangers."

Savannah's pretty eyes gazed at him somberly. "Then that means probably somebody here in town is killing those people. Somebody we know. Maybe somebody we trust."

Once again the knot in his chest constricted tighter. "Hopefully when we get back to the office Dalton will have some answers for us."

Savannah wrapped her slender fingers around her coffee cup and stared out the nearby window. As she looked outside, he found himself staring at her.

She was right. She wasn't beautiful in the traditional sense. But she was pretty, and when she smiled she exuded a warmth that was entrancing.

Today she was dressed in a pair of navy slacks and a pink and navy striped sweater that intimately hugged her curves. As he stared at her, desire struck him like a punch to the gut.

He liked her. The sudden knowledge surprised him. In the time they had spent together he'd definitely come to admire her intelligence, he enjoyed her sense of humor and sensed they shared the same moral standards.

He'd even grown to like the fact that she'd never met a silence she couldn't fill and had come to realize that her stubbornness was actually a fierce determination to do what she thought was right.

There was a soft vulnerability in her that touched him. Even though she often joked about her mother and the ugly things she'd been told about herself, he sensed she carried deep scars from her childhood and it surprised him that there was a part of him that wanted to heal those scars.

He wanted her again. Right here. Right now. He wanted to strip that sweater over her head and kiss the freckles on her shoulders. He needed to hear her soft sighs as he caressed her skin.

She looked at him then and a small gasp escaped her. A blush worked up her neck and swept to her cheeks…as if she were privy to his innermost thoughts, as if his desire was raw and bare in his gaze.

"What are you thinking?" she asked, her voice a husky whisper.

"I was just thinking that maybe after we see what Dalton finds, you'd like me to fix you some lunch at my place." Of course, that hadn't been what he'd been thinking. His thoughts hadn't been of food, but rather of her.

"I'd like that," she said simply, her eyes simmering with unspoken words.

"Don't you want to know if I can cook or not?" he asked.

Her smile heightened the tension and made him glad he was seated at a booth. "I don't care if you can cook or not."

Her reply let him know she was aware of what would happen if she came to his place, she was not only aware of it but apparently wanted him as much as he wanted her.

She cleared her throat and sat back in the seat. "So, you still think it's possible Lauren is after me?"

Thoughts of their lunch date instantly disappeared from his head. "I don't know. I still haven't been able to make contact with her and I have to admit that worries me a little."

He took another sip of his coffee and frowned thoughtfully. "I can't believe how badly I screwed that up."

"From what you told me about the situation, you didn't screw up. It sounds to me like Lauren had some major problems to start with." Savannah leaned forward. "I've never understood those kind of women who smash car windows or rip up clothing or stalk a man because of unrequited love. If a man doesn't want me, then I certainly don't want to be with him. Life is too short for that kind of drama."

"Yeah, but I should have seen that Lauren wasn't right. Somehow I missed the signals, I misjudged her. Reading people and situations is part of what I was trained to do as a bodyguard." Frustration edged through him at thoughts of Lauren.

She reached across the table and touched the back

of one of his hands. "Joshua, stop beating yourself up. If disturbed or evil people were so easy to pick out then we'd know who in this town was responsible for those deaths just by looking at his face. Besides, as far as I'm concerned you're a terrific bodyguard. You saved me from getting a butt full of birdshot, didn't you?"

He turned his hand and grabbed hers as he thought of that moment when Jim Ramsey had told him somebody had been attacked at Winnie's place. "Yeah, but somebody almost beat you to death in your bed and I was nowhere around."

"You aren't to blame for that. Who knew that anyone would break into Winnie's. You can't be with me every minute of the day and night." She released his hand. "Joshua, if I had to handpick a bodyguard, you'd be who I'd choose."

"Why? Because I'm a West?"

"I wouldn't care if your name was Mud." She leaned back in the booth and eyed him intently. "I've seen the way you are when we're out in public, the way you look at everything and everyone, how you measure the safety of the place and the people around me. I'd hire you because whenever I'm with you I feel safe."

Her words dug deeply into him, touching him more than he wanted her to know. "Thanks, and personally I'm glad my name isn't Mud."

She smiled. "You think we should head back over to the office?"

"Yeah, let's go see if Dalton has managed to get us some answers."

Together they left the café and walked the short distance back to the Wild West Protective Services office. Dalton was waiting for them, a frown etched across his forehead.

"I have something for you, but it isn't much," he said. "I can't find anything on the two men, but the address comes back with a listing for a MoTwin Corporation."

"Did you find out anything about the corporation?"

Dalton shook his head. "All I've managed to learn so far is that it's a privately owned corporation. It's going to take me longer than twenty minutes to get more information. It looks like it might be some sort of dummy corporation."

"Keep digging, would you?" Joshua asked.

"Definitely. I'll keep you posted on what I find out."

Once again Joshua and Savannah stepped outside into the late morning sunshine. "So, what do you want to do now?" he asked Savannah. "Do you need to check in at the newspaper office or anything?"

She shook her head, her hair glinting like fire in the sunlight. She looked at him, her amber eyes blazing more gold than brown. "How about that lunch you offered me? I'm suddenly ravenous."

Chapter 11

Not a word was spoken as Joshua sped to the West ranch. Savannah knew they were going to his cabin for one reason and one reason alone.

To make love.

The air between them snapped and crackled with their intent, with their desire for one another. It was as if the electricity was so big, so intense it left no room for talk or thought.

Even though she knew there was no future with him, even though she knew she'd never be anything but a momentary diversion in his life, no doubts entered her mind, her heart. She would take whatever pieces Joshua was willing to give her of himself.

She'd take from him until he tired of her then she

would go quietly away. No drama, no tears. She was the queen of reality, and she had never questioned that her future would ultimately be a lonely one.

They flew by the West ranch house and down a pasture lane, eventually stopping in front of a small cabin half hidden by lush trees and overgrown brush. The place held a rustic charm that wasn't lost on her. It looked like the perfect place for a private midday rendezvous.

Savannah's body nearly sang with anticipation as they got out of the truck and she followed Joshua across the small porch and to the front door.

She'd barely gotten inside the door when he grabbed her and crashed his mouth to hers. The kiss felt half-angry, demanding and all-consuming.

She returned it with the same emotions. She was half-angry with him because she knew that he wanted nothing more from her than to sate a physical desire. She demanded that he give her all he was capable of giving because she was at least worth that much.

They'd entered into the kitchen and the force of the kiss drove her back against the refrigerator. Joshua leaned into her, trapping her between the cool enamel of the fridge and his hot, hard body.

"What are you doing to me?" he asked, his voice a half growl.

"I don't know, but you're doing the same thing to me," she replied breathlessly.

He slammed his mouth back to hers and ground

his hips against hers. She ground back, loving the feel of his arousal hard against her. It frightened her more than a little, the ease that he could sweep all thoughts out of her mind, how easily he drove her half-crazy with desire.

The kiss ended and he stepped back from her, his chest heaving with deep breaths, his green eyes glowing with a primal energy.

"You make me crazy," he said, his voice a husky whisper. "I can't remember ever wanting a woman like I want you right now."

The admission from him simply fanned the flames that burned inside her. "Joshua, I want you so much it's all I can think about."

He took her mouth again with his, his tongue battling hers in a sensual war. Savannah wound her arms around his neck, melting against him as the heat of his kiss weakened her knees.

This time when the kiss finally ended he grabbed the bottom of her sweater and with one smooth action pulled it up and over her head. He tossed the garment toward a small wooden dining table, then grabbed her hand and pulled her into the bedroom.

She had no opportunity to pay attention to the surroundings. There was only Joshua and her desire for him. She was blinded to anything else.

It took only moments for them to undress and get beneath the sheets that smelled of him. They moved together in a frenzy, the lovemaking fast and furious, and when they were finished they remained in the bed, the afternoon sunshine streaming through the window.

For the first time since arriving Savannah took note of the room. Navy curtains hung at the window, matching the navy bedspread that had been thrown off at some point. A wooden dresser sat against one wall, a photo of the West family on top.

She turned over on her side and looked at Joshua, who was on his back, staring up at the ceiling with a frown cutting across his forehead. "What are you thinking?" she asked softly. She placed a hand on his chest, the thump of his heartbeat against her palm.

The frown disappeared as he gazed at her. "Nothing. At least nothing important."

She held his gaze for a long moment. "Do you miss New York City?"

"Not at all." His reply came quickly. He placed an arm around her shoulder and pulled her closer to him. She snuggled into him, savoring the quiet intimacy of not just their physical closeness but also a momentary emotional one as well.

He released a deep sigh. "Going to New York was a mistake. I realize that now. I want my life to be here, in Cotter Creek. At the time I moved to New York I had a need to get away from here, find a place, an identity that was all my own. It's great having a big family, but I needed to get off by myself."

"I can't imagine having everything you have here and choosing to leave it all," she replied. "It has to be amazing to know how much you're loved by everyone around you, to have such wonderful support from your family."

"It is wonderful," he agreed easily, "but it's one thing for your family to think you're terrific. I needed to find out what kind of a person I was separate from my family."

He frowned once again. "Everyone in my family told me how smart I was, how competent, but the only job I'd worked was as a bodyguard for a business my father owned. I needed to find out if I was worth anything besides being a West and working for Wild West Protective Services."

"And did you find what you were looking for?"

"The verdict is still out."

"It's funny, you had to leave your family because you had too much love and support and I had to leave mine for just the opposite reasons." As always, a tiny rivulet of pain fluttered through her as she thought of her parents.

He tightened his arm around her. "Tell me about your mother and father. You've mentioned before that they weren't cut out to be parents."

She ran her hand across the muscled expanse of his chest, enjoying the feel of his chest hair beneath her fingertips. "They aren't bad people. To be honest, I hardly know my father. He worked a lot and when he was home he was completely caught up in my mother. There wasn't time for me in his life."

"And your mother?" His hand rubbed her back in

a gentle swirling motion that was both erotic yet soothing at the same time.

Savannah sighed. Thoughts of her mother always confused her. "I love my mother, but I don't like her very much." She propped herself up on an elbow and gazed at Joshua. "My mother is an absolutely stunning woman. Her life before she met my father had been beauty pageants. By the time she was ten years old she'd won over a hundred contests, but I think that world made her worship beauty above all else and unfortunately I didn't fit into her world. Nothing worse for a beauty queen than to have a red-headed, freckle-faced, outspoken, lacking-of-poise daughter."

Joshua smiled and touched the tip of her nose. "I like your freckles." His smile faded as his fingers slid down her cheek, and he caressed the length of her neck.

He leaned forward and kissed her, a kiss of infinite tenderness and quiet passion. Savannah pressed herself against him, returning his kiss with a tenderness and passion of her own.

She wanted him again and it was obvious from his arousal that he wanted her, too. As his hands moved down the length of her, they didn't move with the white-hot fever that they had earlier, but rather this time it was a slow burn that slowly consumed her.

He touched her everywhere with his hands, with his mouth, caressing and tasting and bringing her again and again to the brink of release then denying her with a low wicked laugh.

She returned the favor, loving the fact that when

she touched him low across his belly he groaned and when she licked across that same skin, he gripped her shoulders and groaned her name like a plea.

When he finally entered her, it was a slow, smooth glide into magic. They made love as if they had all the time in the world, as if they knew each other so intimately there was no need to be adventurous or exploratory. They simply moved together in perfect rhythm, giving and taking as naturally as breathing.

As he kissed her, a deep, soulful kiss, she felt the rise of intense emotions filling her. It was so intense tears stung her eyes. Her heart felt too big for her chest and it was in that moment that she realized she'd only been fooling herself.

She'd believed that she could spend almost every waking hour with Joshua and have sex with him and not get her heart involved. She'd thought she was strong enough not to fall victim to his charm. She'd thought she could know the man inside and not care about him, but she'd been wrong.

The truth was, she was falling in love with Joshua West. He liked her freckles. How could she not fall in love with a man who told her he liked her freckles.

Unfortunately, she knew as surely as she was breathing that she was headed for heartache.

Joshua listened to the sounds of the shower coming from the bathroom. He'd taken a quick shower minutes before and now sat at the kitchen table and waited for Savannah to shower and dress.

He had never felt so confused in his life…confused about himself, confused about Savannah. After they'd had sex the second time he'd looked at her and wondered how anyone could ever even imagine that she wasn't beautiful.

And that had scared the hell out of him. She was creeping in where no other woman had ever been…into his head, into his heart.

At the moment all he felt was a need to run, to escape her with her charming chatter and innate warmth. He needed to distance himself not only from his desire for her on a physical level, but also an emotional level as well.

Despite her background with her family, he thought she was the most together woman he'd ever met. She seemed to know exactly who she was and what she wanted from life and he envied her that.

She'd shown him some of the scars that had been left by her mother and as the youngest son of a loving family, he'd ached for her pain, a pain he'd never known.

He tensed as he heard the shower water shut off. He looked at his watch, surprised to realize how late it had gotten. They had spent the entire afternoon in bed.

There was a part of him that wished they could just grab a bite to eat from the refrigerator, then tumble back into each other's arms and sleep together through the night. But there was a bigger part of him that needed to get away from her.

She was supposed to interview Sheila in less than an hour. He'd take her to the café for the interview, then take her home and tomorrow he'd be stronger where she was concerned.

He had to get control of his feelings, because until he knew where he was going with his life, he had no intention of taking anyone along with him.

He was still seated at the table when she came out of the bedroom. Despite his need to control his emotions, he couldn't help the way his heart leaped as she gifted him with one of her wide smiles.

"I can't believe you don't have a hair dryer," she said as she finger-combed her curly, damp hair.

"Yeah, well, that's because I discourage female visitors," he said.

She stopped in her tracks and stared at him. "Oh, forgive me, I didn't realize you were discouraging my presence here when you were driving ninety miles an hour to get me here."

"You're right. I guess I just want to make sure that you understand that nothing has changed as far as I'm concerned." He knew he was being an ass, but he couldn't stop himself. She scared him, his feelings for her scared him and he needed to gain a safe distance. "I just don't want another Lauren situation on my hands."

Her eyes narrowed. "You're some piece of work, Joshua West. How dare you even think I'd be capable of being a 'Lauren situation.'" Her words were clipped and curt with anger.

Her eyes blazed as she stalked across the room to the front door. "You might be all that and a bag of chips to most of the girls you sleep with, but I told you from the very beginning that all I was looking for was a little fun. You're so worried about me wanting more from you, but what makes you think you're so great that I'd want anything more from you?"

She opened the front door, stepped out then slammed the door behind her. Joshua hurriedly followed, instant regret weighing heavily on his shoulders.

As Savannah started walking, short angry strides taking her past his truck, he called after her. "If you're planning on walking back to town you're going to be late for your interview with Sheila."

She paused, whirled to face him, then walked back to his truck and got in. He slid behind the wheel, then turned to face her. "I'm sorry," he said. "I shouldn't have said that."

She looked at him and in the depths of her eyes he thought he saw a whisper of hurt, but she raised her chin in a show of defiance. "Just get me back to town. I have a job to do." She averted her gaze out the passenger window as if to dismiss him.

He started the engine and pulled away from the cabin, sorry that he'd said anything, sorry that he'd obviously hurt her feelings.

They rode for a few minutes in silence, a taut silence that deepened his regret.

"Savannah, I didn't mean for it to sound like I thought you might be like Lauren," he said after several minutes of the impossibly strained silence. "I just don't want there to be any complications, I wanted to make sure you know where I stood with you."

"You've made that crystal clear," she said with marked coolness in her voice. She turned to face him once again. "Look, Joshua, things have somehow gotten out of control between us, with the bodyguard thing maybe we're spending way too much time together. You know what they say about familiarity breeding contempt."

Once again she turned her head and looked out the passenger window. Her breasts heaved with a deep sigh. "I think maybe we need a break from each other. I appreciate the fact that there might be some sort of threat against me, but I'm a big girl. We have the alarm system now at the house and I know to watch my back."

"We're in the middle of an investigation," he protested. "I'm not sure now is the time to change things." He pulled up and parked in front of the café. He cut the engine, then turned to face her. "We're both running a little high on emotion here. Why don't we wait and see what we find out from Sheila before we make any rash decisions?"

"Fine," she replied, and without another word got out of the truck and slammed the door.

Chapter 12

Savannah knew she'd probably overreacted, but the fact that he'd reminded her that he really wanted nothing from her on any level other than a physical one had echoed with old hurts from her past.

For just a moment, with her newly realized love for him aching in her heart, she'd hoped for something more from him. She'd hoped that the gentleness of his lovemaking had indicated a depth of feeling for her, that the passion he'd shown her had sprung from someplace other than his groin.

Don't expect too much from men, Savannah Marie, her mother's voice rang in her ear. *You just aren't the type of woman that men get all gushy and soft about. I'm only telling you this for your own good. I wouldn't want you to hope for anything that you might never have.*

Her mother's words followed her from the truck inside the café where she picked a booth near the back and slid in. A moment later Joshua sat across from her, his forehead wrinkled with a frown.

"Savannah, I didn't mean to make you mad." There was a plea in his deep green eyes.

How she wanted to hang on to some anger, how she longed to raise her anger like a shield against her feelings for him. But, as hard as she tried, she couldn't sustain her irritation. How could she be angry with him for simply reiterating his rules for their relationship?

She sighed, a new burst of love for him swelling in her chest. "I'm not mad. Let's just forget it, okay?" She glanced at her wristwatch. "Sheila should be here any minute and I need to gather my thoughts for my interview."

She felt incredibly vulnerable and desperately needed some time alone, but she knew he wanted to be here when she spoke with Sheila.

The waitress arrived at the table and both of them ordered only drinks, knowing that they would be eating when Sheila arrived. As they waited for the Realtor to arrive, the silence between them grew uncomfortably taut.

For the first time in her life Savannah felt no desire to fill the silence with talk. Instead she wrapped it around her like a defense against her own feelings.

The café was quickly filling with people as dinner-time approached. Laughter rang in the air, along with the clatter of cutlery and the buzz of conversations.

Normally Savannah would find these kinds of surroundings invigorating, but at the moment a headache began a slight pound across her forehead and she just wanted to get this day finished.

She pulled a notepad from her purse and spent the next few minutes making notes concerning the questions she wanted to ask Sheila.

She wasn't really angry with Joshua, she was angry with herself. She had momentarily forgotten what had been drilled into her from the time she could understand language. Joshua hadn't done anything wrong. She had. She'd fallen in love with a man who was emotionally unavailable.

She looked up to see him staring out the window, and she thought of what he'd told her earlier, about what had driven him away from his family and off to New York to find himself.

It was strange how two people as different as them, as different as their backgrounds had been, could share a common goal to discover themselves amid strangers.

Whatever Joshua had needed, he hadn't found it in New York and she had a feeling until he found whatever it was he needed, he had nothing to offer any woman. In any case he'd made it clear he had nothing more to offer her.

She sat up straighter in the booth as she saw Sheila's luxury car pull up in front of the café. It was the first time she could remember actually looking forward to talking with the abrasive, pushy woman.

"Here she comes," Joshua said as Sheila burst through the front door of the café. Savannah breathed a sigh of relief. It was time to focus on what was important, on what she did best. It was time to interview a woman who might know something about what was going on in this town. At least this was something she did well.

"Savannah, darling, I'm so excited to be here," Sheila said as she reached the booth. "And Joshua, I'm really not surprised to see you as well. The gossip mill has been working overtime about the fact that you two have been joined at the hip since you came home."

Joshua stood and indicated that Sheila slide into the booth opposite Savannah where he had been sitting. "Savannah and I don't pay much attention to the gossip mill," he said.

Savannah thought he might move to another booth or table and leave her alone with Sheila, but instead he slid in beside Savannah, his warm thigh pressing against hers. He obviously intended to be present during the interview.

"I'm just so excited to be here," Sheila said again as she got settled in the booth. "I just love your column and can't believe you're going to write about little old me." As she talked, her long dangling earrings bounced against the shoulder of her rhinestone-bedecked red jacket.

"Shall we order some dinner before we officially begin?" Savannah asked.

Sheila winked at her. "There's two things I love, closing on a great real estate deal and eating." She raised a hand to gesture for the waitress.

As they waited for their orders Savannah and Sheila small-talked about upcoming events in town while Joshua sat silently, invading Savannah's thoughts with his mere presence.

"Lovely wedding the other day, wasn't it? Imagine Clay going all the way to Hollywood to find a bride," Sheila said.

"Yes, it was a lovely wedding," Savannah agreed. She tried not to remember that it had been the day of the wedding that she and Joshua had first fallen into bed together.

The small talk continued as they ate, and it was only when their dishes had been cleared and fresh coffee poured that Savannah got down to business.

She opened her notepad, pen ready. "I always like to start an interview by asking, what are the two things you'd like the people of this town to know about you that they might not already know?"

Sheila frowned and reached up to twirl a strand of her bleached blond hair. "Oh my, I never thought about it before. I suppose I'd like everyone to know that everything I've achieved in my life has been from damned hard work and long hours. And the other thing is that I know I dress flashy and gaudy, but when I was poor and growing up I always said when I got money I'd dress to please myself, and there's nothing I love better than gaudy flash."

"Tell me about your childhood. You grew up right here in Cotter Creek, didn't you?" Savannah asked.

"Right out there on Route 10."

As Sheila launched into the story of her past as one of four children of a dirt-poor rancher, Savannah tried to keep her attention focused on the interview and not on the man beside her or the questions she really wanted to ask Sheila.

There was no point in thinking about Joshua, and it was far too early in the interview for her to start hitting Sheila with hard questions.

People stopping at their booth to greet them interrupted them more than once, but the visits were brief as the visitors realized Savannah was conducting official newspaper business. If there was any doubt about what she was doing, Sheila was quick to inform everyone that she was being interviewed for Savannah's column.

As the questions and answers went on, Savannah felt Joshua's growing impatience and knew he wanted her to get where he wanted her to go. But, Savannah knew the importance of building trust and she wasn't going to allow Joshua's impatience to make her rush things with Sheila.

By the time Savannah decided to heat things up, her headache had fully blossomed, squeezing across her forehead like a vise.

"You ever go to bed hungry?" Sheila asked.

Savannah nodded and she continued. "I went to bed hungry almost every night as a child and I decided then that I was going to make something of myself, make sure I never spent a hungry moment in the rest of my life."

"The real estate business seems to be booming right now in Cotter Creek," Savannah observed, and she felt Joshua tense as if coming to attention.

"I keep busy, that's for sure," Sheila agreed.

"I'd say you've been more than busy." Savannah flipped through her notes. "According to my research, in the last eighteen months you've sold the Townsend and Nesmith places, the Wainfield and Cochran ranch." Savannah named the other ranches that had been sold due to the deaths of the owners.

Sheila's eyes narrowed slightly. "Well, yes, I was the agent for all those places. Whenever any property in this town is ready to market, I try to be there to get an exclusive."

"Did you ever find it odd that all those men died in accidents?"

Sheila blinked once, twice…three times. "I guess I never thought about it before."

She was lying. Savannah knew it in her gut. The rapid blink of her eyelids and the fact that she averted her gaze from Savannah let her know Sheila was definitely lying.

"Then think about it now," Savannah said. "I find it very odd that all those men died in strange accidents, and you were the agent there to sell their property."

Sheila looked at her once again, a hard glitter in her eyes. "All I do is sell land. That's all I do. When I heard each of those men was dead, I talked to their remaining family members and told them I'd get them the best offer if they wanted to sell. All of them wanted to sell. Nothing strange about it."

Joshua had been quiet throughout the interview process, but he now leaned forward. "Sheila, if you know something about those deaths, you need to tell us now."

"I don't know what you're talking about." Her hand rose to her throat, and once again she blinked rapidly. "I told you, I'm just a real estate agent. All I did was sell those properties. I haven't done anything wrong."

"What is MoTwin?" Joshua asked.

Sheila's face paled, and she looked at Savannah with accusing eyes. "I thought this interview was for your column. You got me here on false pretenses." She grabbed her purse from the booth. "I'm leaving. This interview is over." She slid out of the booth. "I don't know anything and I want you both to leave me alone."

"Sheila, men have died and we think they've been murdered. If you know anything, please tell us," Savannah exclaimed.

The older woman shook her head, then hurried away from the booth but not before Savannah saw a flicker of fear in the depths of her eyes.

"She knows something," Savannah said, frustration making her headache intensify. "She knows something and she's scared." She wondered if she'd have managed to get something out of Sheila if Joshua hadn't been there. Maybe his presence had intimidated her.

"Yeah, well, I don't think either one of us is going to get her to talk. Maybe Ramsey can get something out of her. I'll let him know what we've found out."

Now that Sheila was gone, Savannah was acutely aware of Joshua so close to her side. All she wanted was to escape both the noise of the café and Joshua.

"I need to go home," she said and rubbed a hand across her forehead. "I have a headache and I'm tired."

Joshua scooted out of the booth and she did the same. As they walked to his truck a deep weariness swept over her. It had been a day of sheer emotion.

First the unbelievable thrill of making love to Joshua, then the crash down to earth as he reminded her that basically she meant little to him and finally the tense interview with Sheila.

What she wanted more than anything at the moment was a cup of hot tea and meaningless conversation with Winnie, then the privacy and comfort of her bed.

Once again silence reigned as they drove toward Winnie's place, and once again she had no desire to try to break the silence. The vulnerability she'd felt earlier was back, and she was afraid that if she said anything she might make the mistake of showing Joshua just how deeply she cared for him.

It was he who finally broke the silence as he pulled into Winnie's driveway. He put the truck in Park, then turned to look at her. "I'll contact the sheriff first thing in the morning and let him know everything that we've found out."

She nodded wearily. "I still don't think it's necessary for us to be together every waking hour."

He frowned. "We showed our hand to Sheila. Now isn't the time to make changes."

"No more than I've showed my hand before. I've been ranting and raving about a conspiracy for the last couple of weeks. I'll be fine on my own."

She was determined to get some space from him. "Look, all I plan to do for the next couple of days is go into the newspaper office then back home again. You've gone above and beyond for me and I appreciate it. But, let's be real, we have no idea when we'll have some answers about what's been going on and I certainly don't expect you to be my bodyguard for the rest of my life." She certainly knew better than to expect him to be anything to her for the rest of his life.

"You're right," he said after a moment of hesitation.

She sighed in relief. If he'd fought her on her decision to halt his bodyguard duties she wasn't sure she'd have been strong enough to hold her ground.

"You'll let me know if Dalton discovers anything else?" she asked.

"Of course," he agreed.

She opened the truck door and started to step out,

but paused as he softly said her name. "If you get nervous or scared or something doesn't feel safe to you, you know I'm just a phone call away."

"I know that," she said, then slipped from the truck, wanting to be away from him before she said or did anything stupid.

Joshua watched her until she disappeared through Winnie's front door, then he backed out of the driveway and headed home.

He felt bad. He felt really bad. He knew he'd broken something between them and that no matter what happened in the future nothing would ever be the same where the two of them were concerned.

The closer he got to home, the heavier the weight of depression descended upon him. No matter how much he told himself Savannah meant nothing to him, that she'd been a diversion from reality, he knew he was lying to himself.

The sex between them had been amazing, but that wasn't the only thing that drew him to her. She was intelligent and funny and had a warmth about her that drew people to her. But, he wasn't ready for somebody like her in his life. He wasn't ready for any woman in his life.

As he turned onto the West property, he thought about going back to the cabin. He knew the place would smell like her, that her scent would linger in the bedroom, amid the sheets.

Damn, he couldn't remember the last time he felt

so confused, so unsure of his actions and emotions. She'd twisted him up inside in a way nobody had ever done.

Instead of driving by to get to his cabin, he pulled up out front of the big house and parked. For the first time since he'd returned from New York, he didn't feel like being alone. Judd and Jessie greeted him like old friends, following close at his heels as he went up the porch.

He entered the house and headed directly toward the kitchen where he found Smokey seated at the table, a ranching magazine opened before him.

"Hey, Joshua. What are you up to?" The old man closed the magazine and leaned back in his chair.

"Not much. Where's everyone else?" Joshua sat in the chair opposite Smokey.

"Your dad decided to call it an early night and has already gone to his room, and I think Meredith went out to the stables. You want something to eat? I've got plenty of leftovers from dinner."

"No, thanks. I ate at the café a little while ago."

"Where's your sidekick?"

"I left her at Winnie's."

"So, what's on your mind, son? You got that look in your eyes like you need to talk."

Joshua smiled and shook his head. Smokey knew him better than anyone, just like Smokey knew all the West kids inside and out. He'd always been able to tell if one of them needed to talk, had always known if one of them had burdens that needed to be shared.

"How about a drink?" Smokey got up and went to one of the cabinets and pulled down a bottle of whiskey. He poured them each a healthy splash of the liquor, then added a couple of ice cubes to each glass and rejoined Joshua at the table.

"Thanks." Joshua wrapped his hands around the glass. "I'm thinking about working again for the business."

"It's about damn time," Smokey exclaimed. "I don't know what took you so long to make up your mind."

"I don't know. I guess I needed to sort things out in my head."

"It's in your blood, Joshua. You were born to work for Wild West Protective Services."

Smokey's words shot right to the heart of Joshua's insecurities. "That's what bothers me," he confessed after a moment of hesitation. "The idea that the job is there for me because I was born a West, because it's what the West boys do and it has nothing to do with my capabilities."

Smokey stared at him for a long moment, then took a drink and set the glass back down. "What's the matter with you? Do you really think your father would encourage you to come back to the business if you weren't capable?"

"Maybe," Joshua replied faintly, the single word deepening Smokey's scowl.

"Hell, he loves that business almost as much as he loves you kids. Do you really think he'd jeopardize the company reputation by putting you in position as a bodyguard when you aren't qualified?"

Smokey got up and grabbed the bottle of whiskey from the countertop and carried it back to the table. "Damn boy, what did that time in the city do to you?"

He poured himself another shot of the drink and eyed Joshua intently. "If your daddy had any question about your ability as a bodyguard, he'd put you to work as a bookkeeper or a ranch hand. He would never risk anyone's life by assigning a bodyguard who was inadequately trained, or physically and mentally unprepared."

Smokey's words found the tightness that had been in Joshua's chest for the past couple of weeks and eased it. In his heart Joshua knew the old man was right.

Wild West Protective Services had a stellar reputation. His father had worked most of his life to build a company that was known not only in the United States but worldwide for its security and capability.

Smokey was right. If Joshua wasn't good enough, he'd be the last man his father would want working for him, no matter how thick the blood they shared.

Joshua stared down into his glass. "It feels like failure, coming back here, coming back into the family fold. But I missed you all more than I thought I would." He hadn't realized how heavy the burden of feeling like a failure weighed on him until he'd spoken the words out loud.

"Since when is it a failure for a man to know where he wants to spend his life and who he wants around him? Hell, Joshua, it isn't a weakness to need the people you love. It isn't a weakness to surround yourself with people who love you."

Smokey held his gaze intently. "Does this have something to do with that red-haired chatter box?" Smokey asked. "She got you twisted up inside and doubting yourself?"

"No, it has nothing to do with her." He couldn't help but smile at Smokey's characterization of Savannah. He took a sip of his whiskey and relished the slow burn down to the pit of his stomach, then continued. "It's just that everything has always come easy for me. I don't feel like I've ever had to really prove myself or my worth."

Smokey grinned, the gesture lifting his white grisly eyebrows. "You're right. You were plumb spoiled by everyone and that's a fact. All of us catered to you, you being the youngest and all. You didn't have to work real hard to feel special." Smokey took another swallow of his drink. "Maybe we should have made it a little harder on you, but I suppose there's worse things than being surrounded by people who dote on you."

"Yeah, like having nobody who dotes on you." Once again his thoughts turned to Savannah. What would it have been like to be raised by people who never spoke of your worth, who never made you feel special?

He suspected in most cases it could destroy a

person, but in Savannah he sensed a deep well of
strength, a core of identity that nothing and nobody
could shake. He respected that in her.

He was also surprised to realize that it bothered
him more than a little bit that she so easily had dismissed him, that she'd seemed perfectly content in
keeping their relationship nothing more than a
mutual lustfest.

"What else is on your mind?" Smokey asked,
breaking into his thoughts.

There was no way in hell Joshua was going to
confess that a woman he'd known only two short
weeks was messing with his mind. Instead he found
himself telling Smokey everything they had learned
that afternoon and about their interview with Sheila.

"Have you talked to Ramsey about all of this?"
Smokey asked, his grizzled eyebrows pulled
together in a deep frown.

"Some of it, not all of it. I plan on meeting him
first thing in the morning to fill him in on everything." Joshua finished the last of his whiskey, then
leaned back in the chair. "Whatever this is about,
Sheila Wadsworth is in it up to her neck."

"Sheila Wadsworth doesn't have the imagination
or the guts to orchestrate what you think has been
happening here," Smokey scoffed. "She might be in
on it, but I'd bet you my good leg that she's only a
grunt. Somebody else is in charge. Somebody here in
town."

"And that's who I want. I want the man who is responsible for Charlie's death, for all the deaths that resulted in the sale of that land." A hard knot formed in his chest. "I'm hoping Dalton can find out something about the MoTwin Corporation. I want to know who's running it and what they intend to do with the land."

"If what you believe is true and all those men were murdered, then I'd guess this job is too big for Ramsey, too big for any of the local people to handle. Maybe it's time to get in touch with the FBI."

Joshua sighed. "You're right about this being too big for the local law. Unfortunately, right now all we have is supposition where those deaths are concerned. Knowing what's happening and proving it are two different things. And it's not against the law for a corporation to buy land. Until we have some sort of proof, I doubt if we could get the FBI interested."

"Maybe not officially, but you know we've got some contacts there we could call, some markers that could be cashed in," Smokey reminded him.

Joshua nodded and stood. Certainly over the years of working a variety of bodyguard duties, they had all run into FBI agents. In fact, Dalton had become particularly close to one, a man named Alex Bailey.

"I'll give it a couple of days and see what Dalton can find out about MoTwin, then I'll talk to him about him speaking to that buddy of his in the FBI."

"Sounds like a plan," Smokey replied.

"I guess I'll head back to the cabin. Thanks for the drink and the conversation, especially the conversation."

Smokey grinned. "Hell, boy, I didn't tell you anything you didn't know deep in your heart. I'll let you tell your daddy that you're coming back into the fold."

Joshua nodded, then turned and left. A few minutes later he unlocked his cabin door and went inside, instantly assailed by the scent of Savannah that lingered in the air.

It was a good thing that she'd released him from his bodyguard duties, he told himself. She'd been right. It might take some time to get to the bottom of things and he couldn't spend every minute of every day for the rest of his life in her company.

He wasn't even sure the two attacks were related to what was happening in Cotter Creek. If what they suspected was true and men had been murdered to get to their land, then why had the person who'd attacked Savannah in her bedroom not killed her?

Why had she just been beaten up rather than shot or stabbed? While the thought made his blood chill, it also gave him pause. If the attacker had been part of the land deal, then certainly another murder wouldn't have made much difference in the grand scheme of things.

He sat at the table and pulled his cell phone from his pocket. As he had almost every evening for the past week, he punched in Lauren's phone number. He still couldn't quite let go of the possibility that Lauren was here in town, that she was behind the attacks.

It rang three times, then she answered. He was so stunned by the sound of her voice, for a moment he couldn't find his own voice.

"Hello? Is somebody there?" she asked.

"Lauren, it's me, Joshua." He sat up straighter in his chair. So, she was still in New York. But had she been there on the night that Savannah had been attacked? Or had she been here in Cotter Creek, exacting some sort of sick revenge on him?

"Well, well, a voice from the not-so-distant past. What do you want, Joshua?"

"I've been trying to call you for the past week."

"I took a week-long cruise, went to the Bahamas and basked on the beaches. The best thing I ever did for myself. Why have you been trying to reach me? Are you still out there in Oklahoma?"

He couldn't very well tell her he'd suspected that she might have followed him to Cotter Creek and terrorized Savannah. "Yeah, I'm still here. I just wanted to check in and make sure you were okay. The last time I saw you things got pretty ugly."

There was a long silence, then she sighed. "I'd like nothing better than to forget that night at the restaurant. I'm not proud of the way I acted, Joshua. All I can say now is that I'm sorry and I wish you the best of everything."

He believed her. He had no real reason to, but he believed that she'd been on a cruise and the only thing she wanted was to forget her bad behavior, forget him. He suddenly realized that maybe she wasn't the only one who needed to apologize.

"Lauren, I'm sorry for the way things worked out."

Again there was another moment of silence before she spoke. "It's not your fault you didn't fall in love with me," she replied softly. "But, let me give you a little unsolicited advice, Joshua. Don't sleep with a woman and before you're even out of her bed tell her how much she doesn't mean to you. It makes her feel stupid and worthless, and no woman in the world deserves to feel that way."

A vision of Savannah exploded in his head. Was that how he'd made her feel when he'd reiterated that he wanted nothing from her moments after they had made love?

"Thanks for the advice," he said aloud.

"Goodbye, Joshua. Please don't call me again. I'm moving on with my life."

Before he could reply she'd hung up. He replaced the phone in the cradle thoughtfully. He wasn't sure what bothered him more, the fact that he might have made Savannah feel worthless and stupid, or the knowledge that Lauren wasn't responsible for the attacks on her.

Chapter 13

It was just after nine when Savannah decided to call it a night and go to bed. Winnie had retired a half hour earlier, and for the past thirty minutes Savannah had been sitting alone at the kitchen table.

The sharpness of her heartache surprised her. She'd never expected anything from Joshua and the fact that he'd really offered her nothing shouldn't be so painful. But it was.

Falling in love with him had been the last thing she'd expected, the last thing she'd wanted. But he'd snuck into her heart when she hadn't been looking.

She should have known the moment she met him that he was trouble. She should have never enlisted his aid in her investigation. And yet she knew if she hadn't they wouldn't have discovered everything they had.

She got up from the table and moved to the kitchen window and stared outside. It was an unusually dark night with no moonlight piercing through thick clouds. The darkness mirrored her mood.

The ring of the phone made her jump. She hurried to answer before the blaring noise disturbed Winnie.

"Savannah, it's Sheila…Sheila Wadsworth."

Any weariness Savannah might have felt shot away. "Sheila, what's up?" she asked.

"We need to talk. Just the two of us." Tension was evident in the woman's voice.

Savannah clutched the phone more tightly against her ear. "Just tell me when and where."

"In thirty minutes at Big K's Truck Stop out off old Highway 10. You know the place?"

"Yes," Savannah replied.

"Please, come alone and don't tell anyone you're meeting me. I'm putting myself at risk. I trust you, Savannah, but I don't trust anyone else and you shouldn't either."

"Okay, I'll see you in thirty minutes," Savannah confirmed.

Sheila hung up before Savannah could say another word. Savannah quickly grabbed her purse and her car keys and after scribbling a quick note to Winnie to let her know she'd gone out, Savannah left the house.

It would take her all of the thirty minutes to get

to Big K's Truck Stop, which was a good twenty or thirty miles south of Cotter Creek.

As she backed out of the driveway, she thought about calling Joshua but decided to wait and call him after she heard what Sheila had to say. She knew if she called Joshua and let him know what was going on, he'd insist on coming with her and Sheila had made it clear she wasn't going to talk if Savannah wasn't alone.

Driving out of Cotter Creek, she kept a careful eye on her rearview mirror, making sure that she wasn't followed. She'd told Joshua she knew how to take care of herself, but there was a little part of her that was uneasy meeting Sheila alone.

Still, the important thing was that she suspected Sheila was going to tell her something that would break the investigation wide open. She couldn't risk not agreeing to Sheila's terms.

Besides, she felt somewhat confident in meeting Sheila away from Cotter Creek and any prying eyes that might see them together for this secret meeting. Big K's was a busy truck stop. There would be plenty of people around.

When she got to Big K's, if she didn't like what she saw, she wouldn't even get out of her car. She wasn't stupid and wasn't about to walk into any kind of a trap.

As she drove she couldn't help the fact that her thoughts returned to Joshua. She'd been right to tell him that she didn't want him guarding her anymore.

Her heart couldn't stand the thought of spending each and every day with him by her side.

She didn't want to fall deeper and deeper in love with him, knowing that there was no future for the two of them. Whatever his personal demons, he didn't seem inclined to have any kind of meaningful relationship with any woman.

She still was surprised that in such a short span of time a man could get so into her heart. But Joshua had managed to burrow deep inside her soul, and the length of time she'd known him had nothing to do with the strength of her feelings for him.

She consciously willed thoughts of him away as she drew closer and closer to Big K's. Old Highway 10 was nothing more than a dark two-lane road that was little traveled going from Cotter Creek south. Most of the traffic the truck stop saw came from the north, off a freeway exit.

Adrenaline filled her as she anticipated the meeting with Sheila. Maybe finally she was going to get some answers. Maybe finally she'd know the truth about Charlie's death. "I'm going to get to the bottom of things, Charlie," she said aloud. At least his death had sparked a real investigation.

Big K's Truck Stop sported a huge neon sign announcing hot showers and other amenities for truckers. The parking lot was full of eighteen-wheelers, along with several cars parked in front of the large structure.

Savannah was comforted by the fact that there

were plenty of other people around. What she didn't see as she parked in front of the building was Sheila's luxury car. She shut off her engine, then checked her watch. Nine forty-five. Unless Sheila had changed her mind, then she should be arriving at any minute.

As she waited, she tapped her fingernails on the steering wheel and stared inside the windows to make sure she saw nobody from Cotter Creek seated inside.

She saw nobody familiar and that made her relax slightly. If she'd seen anyone from Cotter Creek inside, she would have had second thoughts about going in. Instead she would have turned her car around and headed back to Cotter Creek.

What was Sheila going to tell her? How many questions could Sheila answer about what had been happening? She checked her watch again, hoping that Sheila hadn't chickened out.

Ten long minutes later she saw Sheila's big shiny car pulling into a parking space two slots over from where she was parked. Sheila was alone and didn't appear to notice Savannah as she got out of her car.

Savannah remained in her car and watched as Sheila went inside. She walked with her head down, her steps short and hurried. Once inside she was seated at a booth, then looked at her watch.

Savannah waited several long minutes, watching the people who came and went, checking out the general area for anything or anyone who looked suspicious.

Only then, when Savannah was certain that Sheila was truly alone and nothing looked dangerous, did she get out of her car and go inside.

The place smelled like fried onions and strong coffee and had an underlying scent of motor oil. Most of the occupants were men with tired eyes and stiff shoulders who barely glanced her way as she walked toward the back where Sheila was seated.

"I'm glad you came," Sheila said as Savannah slid into the seat across from her. "I was beginning to think you might not come."

"I wanted to make sure you weren't followed," Savannah said honestly. "What's going on, Sheila?" She pulled her notepad from her purse.

"No, no notes," Sheila protested, her eyes dark and worried. "Please, I just want to talk…off the record or whatever. I need to talk to somebody and I don't know who else to go to."

Savannah put her notepad back in her purse. "All right, off the record," she agreed.

At that moment a waitress arrived at their table. They both ordered coffee, then waited until they were served before continuing.

Sheila wrapped her hands around her coffee cup and for a long moment stared out the nearby window. When she finally looked back at Savannah her eyes were filled with stark fear. "It wasn't supposed to be like this," she said softly. "It wasn't supposed to be like this at all. People weren't supposed to die."

Savannah didn't say anything. She sensed that Sheila needed to tell her whatever was on her mind without prompting. Patience, she told herself. Patience was always a virtue when conducting an interview.

Sheila raised her cup to her lips, her hand trembling slightly. She took a sip, then carefully placed the cup back on the table.

"I'm scared, Savannah."

"Tell me," she urged. "Talk to me, Sheila. We can get through this together." Savannah felt electrified by the fear that wafted from Sheila.

Sheila released a deep sigh. "It started almost two years ago. I got a phone call from a man named Joe Black. He said he and his partner, Harold Willington were part of a corporation that was looking to buy some land in the area."

Joe Black and Harold Willington were the two names listed as owners of the property. "MoTwin," Savannah said.

Sheila nodded. "All he wanted from me was to compile a list of properties that were owned either by men who lived alone or who might be interested in selling out for a decent price. He promised that along with my usual Realtor cut, I'd receive an additional twenty-five thousand dollars for each piece of property the corporation obtained. He told me to go ahead and approach the people I thought might sell, and I did. I talked to Nesmith and Wainfield and most of the others, but none of them were interested in selling despite the fact that ranch life was a struggle."

"So, what happened next?"

"When Joe Black contacted me again I told him the ranchers weren't interested. He told me to keep trying and he gave me a cell phone number to call. He said I should give the list of names to the person who answered the cell phone."

Savannah's head whirled with the information. "So, you called the cell phone?"

Sheila nodded her head. "I just figured maybe they were going to try a little high-pressure effort. But, soon after that was when they started to die."

Once again Sheila's eyes were filled with fear and she reached for her coffee cup, as if needing the warmth to erase a bone chill. "When George Townsend's place blew up with him in it, I thought it was just what it was reported to be, a tragic accident with a kerosene heater. Then Roy Nesmith supposedly fell to his death from his hay loft, and that's when I started to get a bad feeling."

Once again she raised the cup to her mouth and took a sip. "Then more accidents happened, and I knew something bad was happening, something real bad and that somehow I had become a part of it."

"Why do they want the land?" Savannah asked. "What do they plan to do with it?"

"Build a community of luxury condos and homes. According to what Joe Black told me, it's a multi-million-dollar deal. They already have a waiting list of people from both coasts who want to buy when construction begins."

"And who shows up for closing on these deals?"

"Both Joe Black and Harold have shown up for the closings. They fly in, close the deal, then leave town." Sheila replied.

"Do you think he's doing the killing?"

Sheila shook her head. "No. I think there is somebody else working in Cotter Creek. A local, somebody who knew those men, somebody those men trusted and that's the person who has committed the killings."

Savannah leaned back in the booth, her head working overtime to process everything Sheila was telling her. "Do you have any idea who that person might be?"

Once again Sheila shook her head. "I have no idea. I will tell you this, not only is there a cold-blooded killer somewhere in Cotter Creek, there's also people who know what's been going on, people who are in on this whole deal and hoping to cash in big-time. Joe Black was courted by somebody here in town. He didn't just pull the town of Cotter Creek, Oklahoma, out of a hat."

For a long moment the two were silent. Sheila stared back out the window, her features sagging and looking older than she had when Savannah had first arrived.

A sense of euphoria filled Savannah as she realized she had the answers she'd sought. She'd been right about a conspiracy. She'd been right about the deaths not being accidents. But, the euphoria was tempered by the knowledge that good men had died in the name of turning a profit.

"You know you need to go to the sheriff," Savannah said.

Sheila looked back at her once again, her gaze filled with torment. "What if he's part of it?"

Savannah frowned. Sheila was right. There was no way of knowing if Ramsey might be part of the conspiracy or not. She leaned forward. "I'll tell you what, I'll talk to Joshua and maybe he'll know who you need to talk to, who would be safe to talk to."

Sheila worried a paper napkin between her fingers, tearing it into tiny pieces that littered the top of the table. "I'm going to jail, aren't I?"

"I don't know," Savannah answered truthfully. "Maybe you can cut some sort of deal and avoid any real jail time."

"I swear to God, I never knew this was what would happen. When I realized the men were dying, I didn't know who to tell. I didn't know who I could trust. I was afraid to talk to anyone."

"Joshua will know," Savannah replied.

Sheila nodded. "I've got to get home. I need to talk to my husband about what I've done." She motioned for the waitress to bring them their tab.

"I'll take care of it," Savannah said. "And I'll call you as soon as I speak with Joshua. We'll figure it out, Sheila. You did the right thing, coming to me."

"I should have told somebody after George

Townsend died." Sheila stood and grabbed her purse from the booth next to her. "You can't tell anyone except Joshua that we talked. These people are ruthless, and I don't want to be the victim of a fatal accident."

"I'll call you as soon as I have a plan," Savannah said, then watched as Sheila left.

Savannah remained seated after Sheila had gone. She grabbed her notepad from her purse and made notes about what Sheila had told her.

She'd keep her promise to Sheila and wouldn't write a story, but the notes were for herself, to make sure she forgot nothing. This was huge, bigger than she'd even suspected. So many deaths for luxury condos. It made her sick to think that this might be why Charlie had died.

It was just after eleven when she got back into her car to return to Cotter Creek. She'd been so eager to arrive to meet Sheila she hadn't noticed how little traveled old Highway 10 was. She met no cars as she drove the two-lane road.

Joe Black and Harold Willington. The two names went around and around in her head. Had those two businessmen known that they were acquiring their property through death, through murder? Or had they been ignorant of how their contact in Cotter Creek was getting results?

One thing was sure. If Sheriff Ramsey wasn't in on it, it was far too big for him to handle. They were going to have to get outside help. Joshua would know where to go from here, who needed to be brought in to get the guilty people behind bars.

She slowed and pulled her cell phone from her purse, eager to speak to Joshua about what she'd learned. She punched in his cell number and listened as it rang once then went directly to voice mail.

"Joshua, it's me, Savannah. I just met with Sheila Wadsworth at Big K's Truck Stop off old Highway 10. She told me everything. They want the land for luxury condos. I just left the truck stop and am now headed back to Cotter Creek. Call me as soon as you get this message."

She clicked off and threw the phone on the seat next to her, hoping he'd call back soon. Glancing up to her rearview mirror she saw in the distance the headlights of a car coming up behind her.

The car was approaching fast and she moved over to the right shoulder to give the driver plenty of room to pass her. She frowned and squinted against the glare of bright lights reflected in her mirror.

Her phone rang and she grabbed it from the seat.

"Savannah, what in the hell are you doing?" Joshua's voice rang harshly in her ear. "You should have never gone to meet Sheila without me. What were you thinking?"

"It's okay. I'm fine. I'm on my way home now." She squinted into her rearview mirror. "Dammit," she muttered.

"What? What's wrong?"

"Some jerk is behind me with his brights on,"

she replied. The words were barely out of her mouth when the vehicle slammed into the back of hers, the force of the impact wrenching the steering wheel out of her hand.

She screamed and dropped the cell phone, then grabbed the wheel with both hands in an attempt to keep her car on the road. But, once again she was struck from behind with tremendous force.

The steering wheel spun wildly and her car left the road. In horror she had a flash of trees just ahead and knew she was going to hit them.

The last thing she heard before impact was Joshua screaming her name over the cell phone.

Then nothing.

Joshua heard the splintering sound of an impact. He shouted her name several more times and when she didn't answer he hung up and called Sheriff Ramsey.

As he quickly told Ramsey where Savannah was and that she was in trouble, he raced to his truck. Within moments he roared away from the West property and headed for Big K's Truck Stop.

His heart beat so hard, so fast it felt as if it might explode from his chest at any moment. He'd heard the sound of crunching metal, the sound of breaking glass and he knew she'd hit something.

Right now she could be bleeding to death on the side of a road where it might be minutes, or an hour before another car passed her. Fear sizzled through him, making him feel sick with impotence, sick with torment.

He tightened his grip on the steering wheel, a cold chill seeping through him. She'd seen head-lights behind her. Some jerk with his bright lights on. That's what she'd said.

He tromped his foot on the gas pedal, wishing he had wings to fly to her. Damn her for going off on her own to meet Sheila, but double damn whoever might have caused her harm.

As he drove he punched in her cell phone number, hoping, praying she'd answer, but it went directly to her voice mail. The fact that she wouldn't or couldn't answer sent a new chill coursing through him.

When he reached old Highway 10 he slowed down, his gaze shooting left and right of the two-lane road, seeking any sign of her car.

It was about a twenty-mile stretch between where he was now and Big K's Truck Stop. He had no idea where Savannah had been on this road when she'd made the phone call to him.

Emotion clawed up his throat, tasting like grief, but he told himself there was nothing to grieve about. She was okay. She had to be okay. Somehow she'd had a fender bender and now her phone wasn't working. He just had to find her and she'd be all right.

The stretch of highway was so dark, with no streetlights, no light of the moon cascading down from the cloudy night sky. "Where are you,

Savannah?" he muttered, his gaze flying first to the left, then to the right of the road.

He felt ill, more ill than he'd ever felt in his life. As he tried to find her along the dark, lonely road his mind filled with visions of her.

Her charming freckles, her beautiful smile, the warmth of her curves in his arms, each was a haunting memory that ripped at his heart.

As he gazed into his rearview mirror he saw a flash of cherry red lights illuminating the dark and knew that Ramsey was coming up fast behind him. Ramsey must have jumped in his car the moment Joshua had called. Thank God for that. Surely with two of them searching they'd find her more quickly.

When he looked back at the road he saw her car. It was on the right side, about a hundred feet off the road. The front end was smashed against a tree trunk, the interior light on as the driver door hung open.

Joshua yanked his truck to the side of the road, slammed it into Park and left the cab at a run. He was vaguely conscious of Ramsey pulling to a stop just behind his truck as he raced to the wrecked vehicle.

"Savannah!" Her name tore from his throat as he reached her car. It took only a moment's glance to realize she wasn't in the driver's seat. The windshield had shattered, raining glass on the dash, and the airbag had deployed, but there was no sign of Savannah in the car.

"She's not here," Joshua said to Ramsey as the

sheriff hurried toward him. The fear that had sizzled through him before now exploded into unmitigated terror.

"Maybe she tried to walk to get help?" Ramsey suggested.

Joshua looked around wildly. "Savannah!" He yelled her name with all the power in his lungs. Was she wandering around in the dark? Stunned or injured?

His chest tightened as a frantic sob threatened to erupt. Headlights in the distance appproached at a quick pace, but Joshua paid little attention as he yelled her name again and again. The grass beside the driver door was matted down, as if something had either fallen or been dragged.

The car that had approached pulled up behind the Sheriff's, and Bill Cleaver, a rancher from nearby stalked over to where Ramsey stood next to the wrecked car.

"Somebody hurt here?" he asked.

"We don't know, but it looks like it," Ramsey replied.

"Sheriff, that damn fool Larry Davidson just now practically ran me off the road," he exclaimed, then pointed to Savannah's car. "As reckless as he was driving, he probably made this happen, too. He had to have been either drunk or high. I don't give a damn if he works for the mayor or not, he's a menace on the road."

Joshua stared at Bill. Larry Davidson. Wasn't that the cowboy who had stopped them before they'd gone into City Hall? The man who'd asked Savannah out to dinner?

Had he wanted dinner, or had he simply wanted to get Savannah alone? Was he part of the conspiracy going on in town?

The idea of Savannah wandering around in the dark dazed and hurt was bad enough, but the possibility that she had been forcefully taken from the car was terrifying. The matted grass next to the driver door suddenly took on an ominous tone.

"How long ago did he pass you?" Joshua asked tersely.

"About ten miles down the road, was driving like a bat out of hell in that big blue pickup of his."

The words were barely out of Bill's mouth before Joshua was on the run to his truck. Somehow in his heart, in every fiber of his being, he knew that Savannah was in that blue pickup. Now, all he had to do was find her.

Chapter 14

Pain splintered through her head, a pain so intense she felt like throwing up. Her face hurt, too. As if she'd been burned. With her eyes still closed, Savannah started to raise a hand to her throbbing forehead, only to realize her hand wouldn't move.

She frowned, confusion filtering through the pain. What was happening? Where was she? She opened her eyes and stared down at her hands in her lap. Silver duct tape wrapped around her wrists. What? Why was there duct tape there? It didn't make sense.

As the fog of pain momentarily lifted she realized she was in a vehicle, and she turned her head to the left to see Larry Davidson behind the wheel.

She quickly closed her eyes again, feigning unconsciousness as her brain worked to figure out what had happened, how she'd come to be in a truck with Larry, with her wrists bound.

She'd been at Winnie's and the phone had rung. Sheila. She'd had a meeting with Sheila, then she'd been driving home. She gasped as she remembered the bright lights behind her, the crash into the back end of her car and the out-of-control veer off the road.

"Ah, you're awake," Larry said. He'd obviously heard her gasp as her memory had returned.

She thought about pretending to still be out of it but knew there was no point. Instead she opened her eyes once again and looked at him, trying to work past the pain in her head. "Larry, what's going on? Why did you duct-tape my wrists?"

He glanced at her, then back at the dark road ahead. "Ah, Savannah, this all would have been so much easier if you'd just stayed unconscious. I like you, I like you a lot. I tried to warn you off, tried to get you to stop snooping around."

Savannah frowned, the pain in her head making it difficult for her to think, to process what he was saying. "What do you mean? You tried to warn me off?"

"That birdshot that night at the newspaper office? That was me. I thought maybe I could scare you, but you didn't scare easy."

"Was it you who got into my bedroom and beat me up?" Savannah worked her wrists, trying to get the tape to loosen up.

"Yeah, that was me. I hated to do it, but you were

running your mouth to too many people and making somebody uncomfortable. I was told to shut you up. I was hoping that would do it, but you're one stubborn woman, Savannah."

At the moment she wasn't stubborn as much as she was afraid. Fear whispered just under the surface and she tried to maintain control of it, knowing that to give it free rein would make it impossible for her to think. And she had to figure out a way out of this.

"We knew that stupid Sheila might be a weak link so I followed her tonight," he continued. "What did she tell you with that big mouth of hers?"

"I was interviewing her for my column, that's all."

He backhanded her. The blow was completely unexpected and caught her on the side of her jaw. "Don't lie to me. I might be nothing but a cowhand, but I'm not stupid."

Tears sprang to her eyes and she realized she was in trouble…big trouble. Her fear unleashed itself, whipping through her.

"I imagine she told you about the plans for those high-dollar condos and townhouses. Cotter Creek is going to become the place for the wealthy, a playground in the middle of the country for the beautiful people."

"I don't know what you're talking about," she replied.

He snorted. "Too late to pretend, Savannah. This is the best thing that could ever happen to Cotter

Creek. Whether you know it or not, that town is dying. This deal with MoTwin will put money in everyone's pockets. New businesses will come in and the economy will boom."

"Who's in charge in Cotter Creek? Who is your boss?" she asked, working her hands more frantically in an effort to get free. He was talking to her too freely, and that didn't bode well for her.

"Don't know and don't care. I get a phone call telling me to do a job. I do it and I get a nice cash payment deposited in a Swiss account."

"What kind of jobs?" Savannah asked. Keep him talking, that was her goal. Keep him talking until she could get her hands free or come up with a plan to get away from him.

She'd been on the phone with Joshua when her car had struck that tree. If she could just keep Larry talking long enough maybe Joshua would find her.

"All those accidents you've been investigating, they were my work." As he began to tell her about how he'd committed each "accident," Savannah realized there was no way he was going to let her live.

He was confessing to the murders of half a dozen men, pride deepening his voice as he explained how he had set each one up to look like an accident.

Savannah closed her eyes against the burn of tears, a horrible resignation sweeping through her. Her head still ached with nauseating intensity, she couldn't get her hands free no matter how hard she tried, and she knew Larry was driving her to her grave.

"You won't get away with this, Larry. Sheriff Ramsey will figure it out," she said.

He laughed. "Ramsey is a buffoon, too stupid to know what's going on in his own town."

"So, he's not in on it?"

He laughed again. "Ramsey would be the last person they'd bring into this."

They were out in the middle of nowhere and as he turned off the highway and crossed a cattle guard into a large pasture, she knew that it was possible her body would never even be found.

"Old Charlie, he was a tough one," Larry continued. "We knew no matter how much money he was offered he'd never sell. He cursed me with his last breath."

Savannah's chest ached as she thought of Charlie, as she thought of Joshua and everything that was lost to her. She would never know what it felt like to be loved wonderfully, desperately by a man. She would never know what it felt like to look into a man's eyes and see her own soul reflected back to her.

According to her mother, she hadn't been worth much in life and she certainly wouldn't be worth much in death. Suddenly she was angry. Her mother's words had been poison, making Savannah accept less all her life because she hadn't believed she was worth more. She'd always gotten what she'd expected, because she'd never expected more for herself.

Even though she'd always told herself her mother's criticism had fallen on deaf ears, she recognized now the depths that the cuts of those words had made to her soul.

Damn her mother for teaching her not to expect anything from life, and damn herself for taking those perverse lessons to heart.

The weary resignation that had momentarily gripped her was shoved aside by a rage, the likes of which she'd never known.

Dammit, she was worth something, worth far more than she'd gotten from life so far. She wasn't about to just allow this murdering cowhand to take her off somewhere and destroy not only her life but also any dreams she might have harbored for her future.

She couldn't let that happen. Frantically she worked her hands, rubbing them against each other, pulling in an effort to break the tape. She couldn't wait for Joshua, who might never find her. She couldn't wait for anyone to ride to her rescue.

She wanted to survive and promised herself that if she did she would expect more, demand more from life because she was worth it all.

When there was no give to the duct tape, and she knew there was no way she was going to break the bonds, she realized there was only one thing she could do.

Although he was moving across the pasture at a high rate of speed, she knew she had only one chance. Twisting her body, she gripped the door handle, yanked it open and bailed out.

"Hey!"

She heard Larry's outcry just before her body made contact with the ground. She bounced and skidded, pain ripping through her as the air left her lungs and she finally slammed one last time onto the hard earth.

For a brief moment she lay on the ground, trying to find her breath, knowing that if she didn't move she'd be dead. She hurt. Oh God, she hurt so badly. Every bone in her body, every muscle screamed with the abuse they had just received.

As Larry pulled his truck to a stop in the distance, she rose unsteadily to her hands and knees, fighting past the pain. She had to get away. She had to move! She crawled forward, her movements awkward with the duct tape still on her wrists. Sobs ripped through her.

His truck was parked in the opposite direction, the lights beaming away from her. As she moved across the pasture, she prayed the cloudy night would work to her benefit and Larry wouldn't see her.

"You might as well give it up, Savannah." His boots rang against the hard ground. "As much as I like you, I can't let you leave here alive. I got my orders."

She heard the unmistakable click of a bullet being chambered. She swallowed her sobs, afraid the sound would draw him to her. She didn't know whether to lie flat and hope the grass might hide her or keep crawling, knowing that a moving target was harder to hit than a still one.

It was a game of hide and seek in the dark, a game with deadly consequences. If he found her she would die. There was absolutely no way she could talk him into sparing her, no way he'd allow her to live.

She brought her hands up to her mouth and frantically tore at the duct tape with her teeth. Crazy hope filled her as she ripped and gnawed at the tape, finally getting it off her wrists.

At that moment the clouds parted and a shimmering shaft of moonlight drifted down, giving her a perfect view of Larry. And Larry a perfect view of her.

The light glimmered off the gun that he raised, pointing it right at her. A wrenching sob escaped her as she said a quick prayer.

The roar of an engine filled the air and twin headlights bounced into view. Larry spun around and pointed the gun at the approaching vehicle. He fired and glass shattered. He only got off one shot before the truck struck him.

There was a sickening smack, then his body flew into the air. The truck engine stopped at the same time Larry's body hit the ground.

Silence.

Savannah stared at the silent, familiar black pickup. Joshua. With every ounce of strength she had left she struggled to her feet at the same time the driver door opened and Joshua stepped out.

"Savannah! Thank God." He ran to her and wrapped her in his arms. She felt the tremble of his body against hers and the sobs she'd held back in an effort to save her own life exploded out of her.

"Shh, it's all right now. You're all right," he soothed her. He was still holding her when Sheriff Ramsey arrived moments later.

Joshua insisted he take her to the hospital, that any questions Ramsey had for them could wait until Savannah got medical treatment.

But, Savannah refused to leave until she'd told Sheriff Ramsey everything that she'd learned from Sheila and everything Larry had told her. She needed to tell them all of it, while it was still so fresh, so horrifying in her mind.

She held herself together for the telling, although more than once as she shared the details the press of tears burned hot at her eyes.

By the time she'd finished talking to the sheriff one of his deputies had arrived and it was he who drove Savannah to the hospital while Joshua remained behind to answer questions about Larry Davidson's death.

It was only when she was safe in the deputy's car that the full horror of what had just happened descended on her once again.

She wept silent tears, tears for Charlie and for all the other ranchers who had fallen victim to Larry and the crazy land scheme. She cried for Joshua, who had killed a man to save her life.

Finally she cried for herself, because somehow in those moments of facing death she knew she'd been forever changed, and she didn't know whether to weep for what she'd lost or celebrate what she'd gained.

It was just after three in the morning when Savannah sat in the emergency room exam room waiting to be released. She'd been checked over head to toe and had suffered a mild concussion, some facial abrasions from the air bag deployment and a variety of bumps and bruises, but thankfully nothing more serious.

Even though her injuries were minor, her entire body ached from the jolt it had taken when she'd jumped out of Larry's pickup. She was beyond exhaustion and just wanted to go home.

She looked up as the curtain moved aside and Joshua came into the small examining cubicle. He looked as exhausted as she felt with his eyes dark and hollow.

"Hey," he said.

"Hey yourself."

"The doctor told me you're going to be okay," he said.

She forced a smile to her lips. "It takes more than a murderous cowhand to get me down."

"It's not funny," he exclaimed, his forehead wrinkled with a scowl. "When I think about how close you came to being killed, it makes me crazy."

He swiped a hand through his hair, his gaze intent on her. "Have you heard about Sheila?"

"No." Savannah held his gaze and knew. "She's dead, isn't she?"

He nodded. "Ramsey got word that her car was found parked behind Big K's. She'd been shot once in the head."

The news didn't surprise Savannah, although she was sorry to hear that Sheila had been killed in such a brutal manner. "Do they think Larry did it?"

"Right now Ramsey doesn't think so. He doesn't think Larry would have had time to take care of Sheila then come after you."

"So, there's another murderer running loose around town."

"We're calling in the FBI. With the information Larry told you, Ramsey has agreed that he needs more resources than his department has to offer."

"That's good. Maybe finally somebody can get to the bottom of all this." She slid off the table and stood, wanting nothing more than to go home and put this night behind her.

Joshua took two steps toward her and wrapped his arms around her, his heartbeat strong and sure against her own. He didn't speak for several long moments, but simply held her tightly.

She leaned her head against his chest, welcoming the embrace that helped to banish the last of the horror that had clung to her.

"When I saw your car on the side of the road, I

thought I'd die." He stiffened his arms around her, pulling her even more tightly against him.

"I don't even remember hitting the tree," she murmured into his chest. "The last thing I remember is your voice screaming my name from my cell phone."

"Come home with me, Savannah. Let me take you to my place. I want to hold you through the rest of the night." His words were soft in her ear, words that should have brought her a flush of happiness, but they didn't. Rather they caused her pain.

She knew what he was offering. He was asking her for just another single night, a night of him holding her and them making love and then he'd let her go once again.

She might have been tempted before to indulge herself in accepting what little he offered. But, she wasn't tempted now.

She clung to him another moment longer, breathing in the scent of him, allowing her heart to fill with the love she felt for him, then reluctantly stepped back out of his embrace.

"I can't do that, Joshua. I can't do it anymore." She consciously willed away the sting of tears that burned in her eyes as she looked at him. "I've made the very foolish mistake of falling in love with you, and I can't pretend anymore that what you're offering me is enough."

She stepped back and leaned against the examining table, weary beyond words but praying for the strength to do what needed to be done where Joshua was concerned. "Before tonight it was enough. I was willing to fall into your bed whenever you wanted me and not expect more because I didn't think I deserved more. But something happened tonight when I thought I was going to be killed. I realized I'm worth having it all."

Emotion pressed tightly against her chest and she realized there had been a little bit of hope inside her, a piece of her that longed for him to take her back in his arms and tell her he loved her, too. She'd wanted him to say that tonight had changed him as well and now he recognized her worth and wanted more than anything to commit to her. But, he remained silent, his expression inscrutable.

"I deserve to have it all," she continued, fighting the growing need to cry. "I'll find me a lonely cowboy who loves me passionately, who is willing to commit his life to me. He'll love me not in spite of the fact that I talk too much and have freckles and am stubborn, but because of those things."

Joshua shoved his hands in his pockets, his gaze holding hers intently. "You're right. You deserve all that and more. And I hope you find it."

Those words broke what little sliver of hope she had inside her. He was letting her go and even though it let her know her decision had been the right one, it didn't make it hurt any less. At that moment the nurse appeared with her discharge papers.

"You need a ride home?" Joshua asked.

"No, thanks, I'll be fine." She had no idea how she'd get home, but she didn't want to spend another minute with him. Her heartache was too intense and she didn't want to cry in front of him.

He paused a long moment, his gaze intent on her, then he turned on his heels and left the examining room, taking a piece of her heart with him.

"What did you do? Let the dog chew on your hair?" Joshua stared at his sister across the kitchen table. He'd stopped into the big house that morning because he'd found the silence, the loneliness of the cabin oppressive.

Meredith shot a hand up to her dark crooked bangs. "I just trimmed it up a bit." She narrowed her eyes. "My bangs will grow out, but what is it going to take to get you out of your foul mood?"

"I'm not in a foul mood," Joshua replied with a scowl.

"You've been cranky and hard to live with for the past week," Meredith countered.

Joshua knew she was right, and he could identify the exact moment when his bad mood had descended. It had been exactly six days ago when Savannah had told him she was through with him.

It had been a busy six days. The town was buzzing with the news of Sheila's death, the near death of Savannah and the conspiracy of the land scheme. The rumor mill had been working overtime as people speculated on who might be involved in the whole mess.

Ramsey had contacted the FBI and was awaiting the arrival of agents to take over the investigation. Savannah had been responsible for hard-hitting news stories in the paper, and Joshua had told his father to put him back on the roster for the family business.

"I'll feel better when I have someplace to go and something to do," he now said to his sister.

"Things have been slow," Meredith agreed. "We've got half a dozen men out working, but nothing new has come in for weeks."

Joshua finished his coffee and stood, too restless to sit at the table and make small talk. "I think I'll head into town, maybe visit a bit with Clay and Libby." The newlyweds had returned from their honeymoon the day before.

"Tell them I said hi and I hope they had a wonderful time," Meredith said, then grinned. "If I ever get married I'm not sure I want my honeymoon to take place at Walt Disney World."

For the first time in days Joshua smiled. "I'm sure that choice was more for Gracie's benefit than for Libby and Clay."

Meredith smiled, a misty kind of wistful smile. "Libby and Clay would be happy anywhere as long as they were together. I hope I find something like they have some day." She looked at him for a long moment. "Joshua, I don't know what happened between you and Savannah, but I know she hasn't been the same the past week."

He frowned and tried not to remember Savannah's infectious laughter, her penchant for speaking whatever thought crossed her mind. "She'll be okay. She went through a traumatic event. That always changes a person."

"There's a sadness about her that wasn't there before." Meredith studied him. "There's a sadness about you, too."

"I'm not sad, I'm bored," Joshua replied. "I'll see you later. Tell Smokey and Dad I'll stop by later this evening."

Minutes later as he headed into town he tried not to think about what Meredith had said, but the thought of Savannah being sad killed him.

She was a woman born to laugh, a woman who deserved all the happiness life could offer. "She's not your problem," he said aloud.

With all the publicity concerning the imminent arrival of the FBI, he had no real concerns about Savannah's safety. Too many people now knew what had been going on for her to be at risk.

She no longer needed a bodyguard and that's all he'd really agreed to be to her. Meredith was wrong, he wasn't sad that their relationship had ended. He told himself he was relieved that he didn't have to listen to her anymore, that he didn't feel responsible for her.

Still, by the time he pulled up and parked in front

of Libby and Clay's two-story house, his foul mood had returned.

Savannah sat in her little cubicle of an office, typing furiously on the computer. She was writing her column on Sheila. It would be printed posthumously, but Savannah thought it was important that people see not only the bad side of Sheila but the good as well.

Sheila had sold out her neighbors, her town, but Savannah truly believed the Realtor hadn't been a bad woman at heart. She'd merely gotten caught up in something bad and evil because of greed.

Ray Buchannan poked his head in her door and she stopped typing. "I'm going to grab some lunch over at the café. You'll be here to answer the phone?"

"I'll be here," Savannah replied. In the past week she'd spent all her time either in her cubicle working or at Winnie's.

She had little desire to go much of anywhere in town where she might run into Joshua. She knew just seeing him again would bring back all the pain of loss.

The good news was that since the terrifying night out in that pasture her mother's criticizing voice had been silent in her head. Never again would Savannah hear that voice telling her she wasn't worthy, she didn't deserve true happiness and love.

Eventually she'd find what she was looking for, and in the meantime there was her work to keep her satisfied.

As she heard the front door of the newspaper office open, then close with Ray's departure, she leaned back in her chair and grabbed a candy bar from the bowl on the desk.

She unwrapped it and took a bite, deciding that whoever had said that chocolate was as good as sex was a liar. Chocolate couldn't substitute for the feel of Joshua's skin against hers, the taste of his mouth or the sweet joy of making love with him.

No, not making love, she corrected mentally. She had made love. He'd had sex.

It had been Sheriff Ramsey who had taken her home from the hospital that night, and she'd managed to hold herself together until she was in her bed. It was only then that the tears had come.

She'd told herself that the tears had been those of a woman who'd suffered a horrifying event, that they were the aftermath of fear. But, she knew in her heart that those tears had been for Joshua and her decision to halt whatever relationship they'd had.

Even now whenever she thought of him, she felt a swell of emotion in her chest, a wistful longing that things might have been different.

She now finished the candy bar, tossed the wrapper in the trash, then stared blankly at her computer screen. She had to forget him. She had to stop allowing thoughts of him to consume her.

The biggest news stories of her life were happening right under her nose. As a reporter this should be the most exciting time of her life.

Who would have thought a small town like Cotter Creek, Oklahoma, could be such a hotbed of intrigue and murder? Things could only heat up more once the FBI arrived.

The door to the office *whooshed* open and closed. Savannah stood, intent on going to see who had come in, but before she could move from behind her desk, Joshua filled the doorway of her small cubicle.

For a moment she stared at him in shock, wondering if she'd conjured up his image by her mere thoughts alone.

"Savannah." He spoke her name softly.

"Joshua, what are you doing here?" Her heart squeezed painfully at the sight of him. What could he be doing here? What could he possibly want?

"I want you to interview me."

She stared at him in surprise. "What?"

"You've asked me a dozen times for an interview and now I'm agreeing to it." Tension rolled off him and the air between them snapped with energy.

"I don't think I can use an interview now. There's news happening every day. I'm sure you've heard the FBI is going to be taking over the investigation and Sheriff Ramsey has officially announced his upcoming retirement. I've got more stories than I can use at the moment." She was aware that she was rambling and couldn't seem to stop herself.

He was killing her, looking so fine in his tight, worn jeans and navy knit shirt pulled tautly across his broad chest. He was killing her with a softness that radiated from his beautiful green eyes, a softness she didn't understand and was afraid to trust.

"Stop chattering and get out one of those notepads of yours because I want you to take notes," he commanded.

She grabbed a pad and a pen, wondering if something else had happened in town that he was here to report. She sat back down at her desk, then gazed at him expectantly.

"Now, ask me what's in my heart," he said. She looked at him in surprise, the pen poised above the pad. "Go on, ask me."

Her mouth was suddenly unaccountably dry and her heart banged an unsteady rhythm. "What's in your heart, Joshua?" The words came out in a mere whisper.

"You told me once that you'd probably never have a man be passionate about you. Well, you were wrong." His gaze burned into hers. "I feel passionately about you, and love for you is what's in my heart."

She stared at him, wondering if somehow she'd only imagined the words that had just come out of his mouth. The pen fell from her fingers and rolled off the desk to the floor.

"I've spent the last miserable, lonely week trying to forget all about you, trying to ignore what I really felt," he continued, his voice thick with emotion. "The problem was never if you deserved me, but if I deserved you. I came home from New York feeling like a failure, believing that I didn't deserve anything good."

"You aren't hearing my mother's voice whispering in your ear, are you?" She couldn't help it, she had to say something to ease the darkness that momentarily swept into his eyes.

He grinned then, that slow, sexy smile she loved. "No, I'm not hearing your mother. And over the course of the last week I've realized that I'm worth your love and I'm worth the happiness that you give me. I realized that I'm the lonely cowboy who wants to wake up with you every morning, who wants to go to sleep at night with you in my arms. And if you don't get up from that desk and jump into my arms right now, I'll be the most miserable man in the world."

She jumped up from the desk and threw herself at him, her heart so full she couldn't speak for a moment. His arms enfolded her and as she looked up at him, his lips took hers in a kiss that held not just her love, but his.

"This is the best interview I've ever conducted," she said when the kiss ended.

He laughed and pulled her closer. "I love you, Savannah Clarion. I think you're the most beautiful woman in the world. I love your freckles and your chatter. I want you in my life for as long as you'll have me."

"Did anyone ever tell you that you talk too much,

Joshua?" she teased. "Why don't you just be quiet
and kiss me again."

"I'm happy to oblige," he replied, and he did and
in that kiss Savannah realized all her hopes, all her
dreams for a future filled with passion and with love.

* * * * *

Chapter 1

There was something about a parking structure that always made her feel vulnerable. In broad daylight she found them confusing, and most of the time she had too many other things on her mind. Squeezing in that extra piece of information about where she had left her vehicle sometimes created a mental meltdown.

At night, when there were fewer vehicles housed within this particular parking garage, she felt exposed, helpless. And feelings of déjà vu haunted her. It was a completely irrational reaction and as a physician, she was the first to acknowledge this. But still…

Wanting to run, she moved slowly. She retraced

steps she'd taken thirteen hours ago when her day at Patience Memorial Hospital had begun. The lighting down on this level was poor, as one of the bulbs was out, and the air felt heavy and clammy, much like the day had been. Typical New York City early-autumn weather, she thought. She picked up her pace, making her way toward where she thought she remembered leaving her car, a small, vintage Toyota.

Dr. Sasha Pulaski stripped off her sweater and slung it over her arm, stifling a yawn. The sound of her heels echoed back to her. If she was lucky, she could be sound asleep in less than an hour. Never mind food, she thought. All she wanted was to commune with her pillow and a flat surface—any flat surface—for about six hours.

Not too much to ask, she thought. Unless you were an intern. Mercifully, those days were behind her, but still in front of her two youngest sisters. Five doctors and almost-doctors in one family. Not bad for the offspring of two struggling immigrants who had come into this country with nothing more than the clothes on their backs. She knew that her parents were both proud enough to burst.

A strange, popping noise sounded in the distance. Instantly Sasha stiffened, listening. Holding her breath. Memories suddenly assaulted her.

One hand was clenched at her side, and the other held tightly to the purse strap slung over her shoulder. She willed herself to relax. More than likely, it was just someone from the hospital getting into his car and going home. Or maybe it was one of the security guards, accidentally stepping on something on the ground.

In the past six months, several people had been robbed in and around the structure, and as a result the hospital had beefed up security. There was supposed to be at least one guard making the rounds at all times. That didn't make her feel all that safe. The hairs at the back of her neck stood at attention.

As she rounded the corner, heading toward where she might have left her vehicle, Sasha dug into her purse. Not for her keys, but for the comforting cylindrical shape of the small can of mace her father, Josef Pulaski, a retired NYPD police officer, insisted that she and her sisters carry with them at all times. Her fingers tightened around the small dispenser just as she saw a short, squat man up ahead. He had a mop of white hair, a kindly face and, even in his uniform, looked as if he could be a stand-in for a mall Santa Claus.

The security guard, she thought in relief, her fingers growing lax. She'd seen him around and even exchanged a few words with him on occasion. He was retired, with no family. Being a guard gave him something to do, a reason to get up each day.

The next moment, her relief began to slip away. The guard was looking down at something on the ground. There was a deep frown on his face and his body was rigid, as if frozen in place.

Sasha picked up her pace. "Mr. Stevens?" she called out. "Is something wrong?"

His head jerked in her direction. He seemed startled to see her. Or was that horror on his face?

Before she could ask him any more questions, Sasha saw what had robbed him of his speech. There was the body of a woman lying beside a car. Blood pooled beneath her head, streaming toward her frayed tan trench coat. A look of surprise was forever frozen on her pretty, bronze features.

Recognition was immediate. A scream, wide and thick, lodged itself in Sasha's throat as she struggled not to release it.

Angela. One of her colleagues.

She'd talked to Angela a little more than two hours ago. Terror vibrated through Sasha's very being.

How?

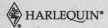

This February...

Catch NASCAR Superstar **Carl Edwards** *in*

SPEED DATING!

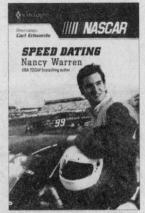

Kendall assesses risk for a living—so she's the last person you'd expect to see on the arm of a race-car driver who thrives on the unpredictable. But when a bizarre turn of events—and NASCAR hotshot Dylan Hargreave—inspire her to trade in her ever-so-structured existence for "life in the fast lane" she starts to feel she might be on to something!

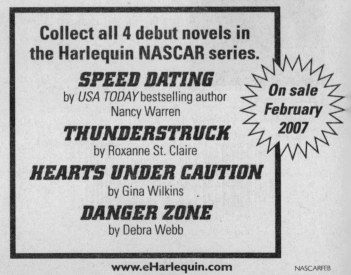

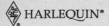

EVERLASTING LOVE™

Every great love has a story to tell™

Save $1.⁰⁰ off

the purchase of
any Harlequin
Everlasting Love novel

Coupon valid from January 1, 2007
until April 30, 2007.

Valid at retail outlets in the U.S. only.
Limit one coupon per customer.

5 65373 00076 2   (8100)0 11302

HEUSCPN0407

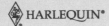

HARLEQUIN®

E V E R L A S T I N G   L O V E™

Every great love has a story to tell™

Save $1.⁰⁰ off

the purchase of any Harlequin Everlasting Love novel

Coupon valid from January 1, 2007 until April 30, 2007.

Valid at retail outlets in Canada only. Limit one coupon per customer.

52607370

HECDNCPN0407

What a month!

In February watch for

Rancher and Protector

Part of the Western Weddings miniseries

BY JUDY CHRISTENBERRY

The Boss's Pregnancy Proposal

BY RAYE MORGAN

Also in February, expect
MORE of what you love
as the Harlequin Romance line
increases to six titles per month.

REQUEST YOUR FREE BOOKS!

2 FREE NOVELS PLUS 2 FREE GIFTS!

Silhouette® Romantic

SUSPENSE

Sparked by Danger, Fueled by Passion!

YES! Please send me 2 FREE Silhouette® Romantic Suspense novels and my 2 FREE gifts. After receiving them, if I don't wish to receive any more books, I can return the shipping statement marked "cancel." If I don't cancel, I will receive 4 brand-new novels every month and be billed just $4.24 per book in the U.S., or $4.99 per book in Canada, plus 25¢ shipping and handling per book plus applicable taxes, if any*. That's a savings of at least 15% off the cover price! I understand that accepting the 2 free books and gifts places me under no obligation to buy anything. I can always return a shipment and cancel at any time. Even if I never buy another book from Silhouette, the two free books and gifts are mine to keep forever.

240 SDN EEX6 340 SDN EEYJ

Name	(PLEASE PRINT)	
Address		Apt. #
City	State/Prov.	Zip/Postal Code

Signature (if under 18, a parent or guardian must sign)

Mail to the **Silhouette Reader Service**™:
IN U.S.A.: P.O. Box 1867, Buffalo, NY 14240-1867
IN CANADA: P.O. Box 609, Fort Erie, Ontario L2A 5X3

Not valid to current Silhouette Intimate Moments subscribers.

Want to try two free books from another line?
Call 1-800-873-8635 or visit www.morefreebooks.com.

* Terms and prices subject to change without notice. NY residents add applicable sales tax. Canadian residents will be charged applicable provincial taxes and GST. This offer is limited to one order per household. All orders subject to approval. Credit or debit balances in a customer's account(s) may be offset by any other outstanding balance owed by or to the customer. Please allow 4 to 6 weeks for delivery.

Your Privacy: Silhouette is committed to protecting your privacy. Our Privacy Policy is available online at www.eHarlequin.com or upon request from the Reader Service. From time to time we make our lists of customers available to reputable firms who may have a product or service of interest to you. If you would prefer we not share your name and address, please check here. ☐

SRS07

Don't miss the first book
in THE ROYALS trilogy:

THE FORBIDDEN PRINCESS
(SD #1780)

by national bestselling author

DAY LECLAIRE

Moments before her loveless royal wedding,
Princess Alyssa was kidnapped by a mysterious man
who'd do anything to stop the ceremony. Even if that
meant marrying the forbidden princess himself!

On sale February 2007 from Silhouette Desire!

THE ROYALS
Stories of scandals and secrets
amidst the most powerful palaces.

Make sure to read the other titles in the series:
THE PRINCE'S MISTRESS
On sale March 2007
THE ROYAL WEDDING NIGHT
On sale April 2007

*Available wherever books are sold, including most
bookstores, supermarkets, discount stores and drugstores.*

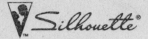
COMING NEXT MONTH

SIMCNM0107